THE DANCE BOOTS

FLANNERY
O'CONNOR
AWARD
FOR
SHORT
FICTION

Nancy Zafris,
Series Editor

THE DANCE BOOTS

LINDA LEGARDE GROVER

The University of Georgia Press
Athens and London

© 2010 by Linda LeGarde Grover

Athens, Georgia 30602

www.ugapress.org

Designed by Mindy Basinger Hill

Set in 10/14.5 Adobe Caslon Pro

Printed and bound by Thomson-Shore

The paper in this book meets the guidelines for
permanence and durability of the Committee on
Production Guidelines for Book Longevity of the
Council on Library Resources.

Printed in the United States of America

14   13   12   11   10   C   5   4   3   2   1

Library of Congress Cataloging-in-Publication Data

Grover, Linda LeGarde.

The dance boots / Linda LeGarde Grover.

    p.   cm. — (Winner of the Flannery O'Connor Award
for short fiction)

ISBN-13: 978-0-8203-3580-3 (hardcover : alk. paper)

ISBN-10: 0-8203-3580-0 (hardcover : alk. paper)

1. Ojibwa Indians—Fiction. 2. Minnesota—Fiction. I. Title.

PS3607.R6777D36 2010

813'.6—dc22   2009051211

British Library Cataloging-in-Publication Data available

TO ALL THE LEGARDES

AND DROUILLARDS

BY BLOOD,

BY NAME,

BY MARRIAGE,

BY SPIRIT

HERE AND AANDAKII

CONTENTS

PREFACE

The mythical Mozhay Point Indian Reservation and allotment lands of the Ojibwe extended families in these stories are in the heart of the six reservations of the Minnesota Chippewa Tribe, a few hours' drive north of Duluth, Minnesota, which is a hill city on the shores of Lake Superior.

The Ojibwe are of the Woodland cultures. Half a millennium ago our ancestors made the journey we call the Great Migration in a route along the Great Lakes from the east coast of North America, near Newfoundland, to our home today. We have maintained and when necessary revitalized our language, history, and customs by way of our oral tradition as well as the determination and sacrifices of those we call the Grandfathers.

Our families are large and extended; we have many relatives. Sometimes we address each other not by name but by relationship (for example, Auntie or Cousin), as a term of affection or unity. At times we do not differentiate between degrees of relationship: all cousins, first-degree and beyond, as well as other relatives of the same generation might be addressed as Cousin; relatives of one older generation might all be addressed as Auntie or Uncle, though they might technically be cousins; some whom we address as relatives may not be actual relatives but are honored with that title. We are all related.

Ojibwe names at times combine English and Ojibwe spelling and pronunciation. The Ojibwe language does not differentiate between the letters *p* and *f*; the letters *l* and *n* can be interchangeable when English language is spoken, as can the letters *l* and *y* and the letters *r* and *n*. Examples of this can be found in some of the names of characters in these stories: Charlotte is called Shonnud, and Helen is called Henen. In every day that passes, this speech pattern is heard less frequently, as elders who spoke both the old Ojibwe dialects and English in the old Ojibwe way pass on to the next world. I remember their way of speaking in these stories to commemorate, honor, and thank them.

THE DANCE BOOTS

THE DANCE BOOTS

We Ojibwe believe that God the Creator has put each of us in the living world with a gift or talent, something that we are supposed to search for in ourselves, thank Him for, and contribute to those we share the world with. We are each born for a purpose, each with tasks to accomplish. My aunt Shirley's was to remember by heart and teach by rote, mine to learn by rote and remember by heart. With Shirley gone, one of these days the time will be right for me to become the teacher. I will choose someone who, like me, might not know, at first, why.

When my daughters were still little girls and we lived in Mesabi, just about an hour from my cousins who lived at Mozhay Point Reservation, my aunt Shirley began to call me long-distance from Duluth, sometimes every couple of weeks, sometimes every couple of months, not much before the ten o'clock news, and after the kids had gone to bed. This was during the years that Stan thought I was the stupidest woman in the world, and so I worked at a series of jobs, sometimes at the hospital switchboard, sometimes at the drugstore, sometimes at the concession stand at the movies, and started to take classes at the community college, too, all to try to show him that I was not a complete zero, except for my drinking, and that wasn't too bad most of the time. When I realized that my drinking was the one thing he liked about me because it proved everything he thought, I pulled myself together and cut down. That was in the middle of Shirley's story, and it made listening harder because without that thick white ground fog of liquor I could hear it so clearly.

When the phone rang I would have dishes to wash, or a load of laundry ready to fold, or a pair of girls' jeans to mend or to hem, and always a reading assignment or a paper to write. My days and nights were spent on the run; I thought sometimes about not picking up the telephone, but I always did because it might be Shirley. She was my aunt; she had something to tell me.

"H'lo?"

"Artense. How are you tonight, my dear?"

"Hi, Shirley. Oh, I'm good. How about you; what are you up to?"

She had bought a pair of knee-high fringed boots to wear with her powwow dress. Oh, that would look nice, I said, with her dark blue skirt and dark red blouse. She wondered, did I want her leggings, since because the boots covered her legs she wouldn't need them? They would go nice with my ribbon shirt, and she thought I could make myself a skirt and we could dance together. Embarrassed that I didn't know how to dance, I told her I thought she should keep them; she might want them in the summer, when her legs might get pretty hot in suede boots.

She had talked to her sister and told her that it was time to stop hanging around the house and start getting out again. Time to get out and see some people. "Says she misses the Russian. Why would she ever miss that old cheapskate, anyway? I told her, 'Well, he's dead, now. Find somebody else!' She was way too young for him, anyway, I told her. 'Find yourself somebody younger this time,' I said! 'Get yourself a boy-toy!'" She found this so funny that she repeated it several times. It took a few minutes for her to stop laughing.

She had driven the Indian Health Services van all the way to West Duluth to give her ladyfriend Mrs. Minogeezhik a ride to the clinic for an appointment. "Mrs. Minogeezhik, you remember her, she was at the Home Improvement Showcase down at the hockey arena, the lady in the wheelchair?"

I was sorting through the pile of newspapers by the back door, looking for the Sunday grocery coupons. "Yes, she was in front of the Mary Kay counter, right? She asked me who my mother and father are." The Mary Kay lady had given Shirley a lipstick sample and looked nervously at Mrs. Minogeezhik's son, Punkin, that grinning charcoal drawing of a jack-o'-lantern shaded and contoured by ground-in grime from his job at the garage and so massive in his size triple-extra-large Carhartt jacket that he blocked one half of the perfumed and cluttered, pristine and pink display counter and shadowed the rest. "Punkin was there, too."

"Remember that time when your Uncle John picked up Punkin's jacket off the back of the chair at your mom's house and said, 'Hey, Punkin, looks like your jacket could use an oil change!' Gawd, we laughed! Everybody always has such a good time at your mom's. An oil change—that John. Anyway, she remembered you."

Where were the cereal coupons? I dug through the Sunday paper. "Who did?"

"Wegonen, my girl? Who did what—oh, remembered you? Mrs. Minogeezhik. She said you have beautiful manners. She thinks you have a handsome husband. Ay-y-y-y."

"Oh my." We giggled. "Now, don't tell him that; he doesn't need to hear it!"

The night the story really started, she called to say that she was having a glass of wine and thinking of me and how I was doing.

"How is everything at college? What is it you're taking there?"

"History. And biology. It's just a couple of nights a week. After work I make supper and feed Stan and the girls and then go right to class."

"White Man history, right?"

"It's called the Age of Exploration."

"It must be hard, eh? But those are all things you need to know. And you're smart; you'll study hard and do good."

"Well, the book is good, and I got an A on a test." I was the only Indian student in the class and over thirty, the oldest person in the room except for the professor. I wanted to graduate, to be an associate of arts, whatever that might be, and with some practice was learning to eat whatever Dr. Morcomb put on the plate. Just that day it had been a lunch of Indian-European relations. Indians had infected early explorers to this continent with venereal disease, which was then brought back to Europe on return voyages and became epidemic, he told us. I snorted, which startled the young man who sat next to me drawing a picture of a pickup truck. *Fire and Ice*, he had written below the drawing. He had drawn decals of snow and Old Man North Wind on the hood and box, flames on the fenders.

"Is that really true?" I asked.

The young man looked at me with respect inspired by fear. I had the power of the clap. Indian Power.

Dr. Morcomb said, "This is actual documented history, researched by scholars. There is documented proof in the form of diaries, and also reports written by physicians themselves."

Being no scholar myself, I took a big spoonful, opened my mouth and held my nose, and swallowed. In the margin of my notebook I wrote, *From the diaries of Cartier: What the hell is this?* CLAP? *I must of got it from that damn Indian!*

The scratching of a match against a strip of roughened cardboard; the nearly invisible sound of flame struck from a red-tipped match; the *pf-f-f-ft* of Shirley inhaling ignited tobacco and paper into her lungs. "Oh, wuh! An A!" A dry cough; a sigh.

"But, my mom says it's no wonder I got an A; it's because I'm so old, I was there when things we're studying happened, she says, and the kids in class weren't even born yet!"

"That Patsy!" She laughed. "But you probably know lots of things those professors don't know! You just tell them if they need educating!"

"Biology's hard, though. They say that almost half the people in the class fail it." It was my second try; did that mean that the mathematical odds were against me, or were they in my favor?

"Don't you let them chase you out of there; that's just what they want. We don't let them do that to us anymore. And do you know why, my dear?" She hiccupped. "It's because we're strong." She paused, sipped, thought. "No, my dear, you're not gonna let yourself get chased out of there. And do you know why?"

"Because we're strong?"

"That's right; because we're strong. You just keep on going; we're all proud of you. Me and your uncle Jimmy, and your dad, he's real proud of you. You just keep on." My dad had been smart in school, she said, smart like me. He was a good speller, the best one in the class, and he used to read all the time. "Does your dad still do that? Does he still read all the time?" He could have gone to college or something like that; things were different then, though. "We were in Catholic school together, your dad and me and your uncle Jimmy, and my sisters, too. They were mean to us there, the nuns; they treated us bad, used to pick on us. They even had the other kids making fun of us; can you believe nuns would do that? Oh, they were mean. But you know? That was nothing compared to what my mother went through, and your grandma Maggie. And Louis, your grandpa, too, there at that Indian school in Harrod. But you know what? They never let that beat them, and you know why?" She yawned. Waited.

"Because we're strong?"

"Because we're strong." The silvery tinkle of a sand-filled beanbag ashtray lifted and set down again; the metallic tap-tap of cigarette against the small aluminum bowl set into the Campbell plaid fabric of the ashtray.

Because I was cutting grocery coupons out of the newspaper while she talked, it took a second for her story to register. "They all went to the Harrod school?"

"Sure, they did; they all did. Didn't you know that?"

"I thought my grandma went to some mission school."

"Yes, the girls all did, your grandma and my mother and Auntie Helen; they went to that mission school, St. Veronique's, way up near Canada, when they were just little girls. Some of those girls went through a lot there, some terrible things. My mother told me. And then for some reason I don't know, after a while they all left there and moved back to Mozhay Point, and then the girls went to the school in Harrod. That's where your grandma met your grandpa, there at Indian school. Didn't you know that? Didn't you? Well, they did, and if it wasn't for that Harrod school, you wouldn't be here! Your grandma Maggie was older than Louis, you know, and she used to work there after she was done with school, and take care of him, when he was a little boy. These are some things you should know." She yawned again, sleepy from the wine. "My dear, I'll let you go to bed."

"Well, you have a good sleep."

"You do the same, my dear." Then she said, "but I'll call you back. I want you to know these things. I want to tell you these things."

That's where the story started. Why she chose me I don't know.

When I was growing up in the 1950s and 1960s, how and where

my relatives had been schooled was rarely mentioned and never discussed. Instead, the education of American Indians prior to my generation was a topic to be avoided, a source of secrecy and loss, with an undercurrent of shame. My uncle George told me, when I was a little girl, that he had gone away from home to go to school. This was a "different kind of school" that he didn't like. He advised me that it wasn't good to think much about the past, that we didn't need anybody to feel sorry for us. I thought that he must have done something wrong, and that he must have been sent to reform school. What could he have done, I asked my mother. She told me that he didn't do anything wrong, that in the time before I was born most Indian children were removed from their homes by the government and sent away to boarding schools. Don't ask him about it anymore, she said; the story made him sad and would make me sad, too, if I knew it, so don't bother him about it; just be thankful for the life I had.

I spent my childhood and teen years protected from the sorrows of the past by its invisible swaddling. School involved more than learning to read and count, more than recess and gym; school also involved trying to walk with dignity through the annual "Indian unit" during Thanksgiving week, trying to play the clown through thoughtless children's jokes about scalpings, trying to displace myself into another dimension when a boy imitated the staggering walk and slurred speech of an Indian man he saw going into a liquor store. I was the oldest child, the Indian scout for my family's foray into public school education; I had a responsibility. I owed it to the past to survive in the present, to the mysterious and heartbreaking experiences of my elders to count coup on formalized schooling: get close, tap it on the shoulder, and run in triumph. I almost did it, but that's another story.

I don't know why she chose me. Maybe she thought I could survive to tell the tale. What I do know is that my aunt Shirley had watched and listened to what was going on around her all of her life, that she had saved and cared for what she had received of others' lives, and that she didn't want the story buried with her when she died. When she began the story, I was in community college and Shirley was driving for Indian Health Services; the last day of the story, that day my dad and I visited her in her trailer, I was in graduate school and Shirley had retired and was dying. Over the last decade or so of her life, she would call, sometimes every few weeks, sometimes after several months, to tell me another part of the story. Eventually, having heard the rhythm and pattern of repeating and echoing, re-echoing and returning, I felt the story taking root in my brain and in my heart and saw that the day was coming that I would continue Shirley's task of listening and watching, remembering, and then doing my part to pass on and continue the story. When she started I was a young mother; when she finished, a grandmother.

In the meantime, Shirley went into treatment twice; to keep her company during her second thirty days of absence, I practiced controlling my thirst and sorrow. The next year, her first year of sobriety, I began to dance. My dress, dark blue with red ribbons, was sent to me by Aunt Shirley in a dream.

The story she told me is a multigenerational one of Indian boarding schools, homesickness and cruelty, racism, and most of all, the hopes broken and revived in the survival of an extended family. From the beginning of her story, when my grandmother was sent to a Catholic mission school in Canada, to the heyday of boarding schools in the 1910s and 1920s, through the 1930s when the Indian Reorganization Act provided money incentives for local school districts to admit Indian children, I experienced through Shirley my family's role as participants in and witnesses to a vast experiment in the breaking of a culture through the education of its young. She would talk for an hour or so, until she had shared enough of our story to become tired and until I had absorbed enough to become sleepless. Drained by the tale and honored with the burden, I lay awake for hours, knowing how hard it was going to be to get up in the morning to get ready for work. To pass the time, I would repeat the story to myself, silently, to the rhythm and drone of Stan's and the girls' snores and sleep sighs. I was learning by rote but not yet by heart.

One morning the feeling of my littlest girl's fine, straight hair in my hands as I braided then crossed and tied her braids in ribbons behind her ears brought to mind that she was the age my grandmother had been when she left home for boarding school, just five years old. I would be walking my own five-year-old to school; we would see each other again that same afternoon after I finished work. I began to appreciate more the struggles and tenacity of my family as well as of all Indian people, whose valuing of family and tribal culture made it possible for people like me to live with our own families and have our children experience an education that is in so many ways so different from that of our grandparents. I began to see that as Indian people our interactions with society and with each other include the specter of all that happened to those who went before us. As their schooling experiences defined too much of their lives, so that legacy continues to define much of ours. Yet without it, we disappear.

The last time we visited Aunt Shirley at home, my dad and I, she was waiting for us and opened the screen door as soon as we got out of the truck in front of her trailer. She stood in the doorway, waving and smiling while we walked over the boards laid over the muddy yard and up the stairs to the vestibule outside the kitchen.

"Buster! Artense! Come in; biindigen! Come on in!"

Above the reddened dryness of her high, high cheekbones, stars rose in delight from the dark, dark depths of her eyes and danced. "Boozhoo, boozhoo! N'madabin; have a chair!"

Her appearance was not shocking: she was thin, and a little pale, like she'd been up all night. And she acted the same, not as though she was dying, which she was, and which was the reason for our visit. This might not have been real. She might have only been dieting, and our visit only social; perhaps her death was not grinning at us from the corner of the room, where he leaned with the patience and anticipation of inevitability. Maagizhaa; maybe.

Her manners were flawless, traditional: She made sure that we had the most comfortable place to sit, on her couch, which she had covered with her good afghan. She accepted the pink-flowered paper plate of peanut butter cookies that my mother had baked that morning and covered with pink Saran Wrap, and she placed it in the center of the dining room table, next to a box of chocolate doughnuts. She offered us tea. She asked how everybody was doing, my mother and brothers and sisters, my husband and children. My dad told her how good her house looked and what a nice place it was. He asked how old was the waterproofing stain on the front steps and said that it looked like new. "Boy, this is a really nice place," he said again.

I offered the plate of cookies to my dad because I knew that Shirley wouldn't take one until he did. "Patsy made these, hey," he said. "You should try one. Boy, they're good."

"My mom said they're supposed to be good for you," I told Shirley. Could she possibly have any appetite, I wondered. Could the cookies help anything as serious as lung cancer? My mother's peanut butter cookies could be magical, healing. They were not too big, not too small, tender in the middle, crisp around the edges, nearly as light as air. On the tongue, they dissolved into grains floating in a sweet and salty cream. She made them often and kept them in a commercial-sized pickle jar on the kitchen table. She packed them in plastic bags that she had my dad drop by relatives' houses when they were sick. They were light on the stomach, she said, and helped keep your strength up. She advised saying a rosary, too.

Shirley picked out the smallest cookie with her fragile hand, which was nearly fleshless, just thin and wrinkled skin over bone, and bit a neat scallop from the edge, chewing daintily with her front teeth. I said a Hail Mary silently. "My, these are delicious," she said, and took another bite.

We brought her a manila envelope filled with photocopies of old pictures. She spread them out on the coffee table, one by one, naming all of the people, until the surface was covered. There was Shirley, a little girl posed with her brothers and sisters in front an elm tree, just half a block from where their aunt, my grandma Maggie, who died before I was born, lived. Shirley's mother, our great-aunt Lisette, and Grandma Maggie posed in a studio portrait with great-aunt Helen and their mothers, sometime in the 1920s. A dozen children, cousins, grouped together next to a picnic table. A hundred boys and girls in uniforms lined up in rows on the steps of the Harrod Indian School, Lisette with the big girls, Louis with the boys, Maggie between the girls' matron and the cook. Shirley in skinny pedal pushers and harlequin glasses holding a little boy in shorts and engineer boots up to face the camera, her ponytail blowing almost straight up in the wind. An old woman in an ankle-length cotton print housedress, Aunt Lisette shaking her finger at the person behind the camera, tucking escaped wisps of hair back into her chignon with her other hand. Shirley in a lawn chair at Aunt Babe's last August, legs crossed, one sandal balanced off her toes, fingers trailing over grass and dangling a cigarette, straw hat casting patterns of sunlight across her laughing face. Her mouth was open; her gold tooth glistened wetly in the light of that late summer day. On the ground next to her was a paper plate of untouched picnic food.

"It's me! Look, it's me!" She held up the copy of a small snapshot of a little girl on a snow-covered porch, smiling into the camera, wearing a knit hood and mittens. "I don't remember this picture! Where did you find all these?"

She was so much thinner than last summer. Her brown hands were twigs, dry and chapped against the freshness of her nail polish as they moved stiffly among the stack of photographs.

"And look at this one; it's Maggie and Dolly. Oh, we used to love to go visit there, when they lived in that apartment in the west end. That Dolly, she was so nice, everybody liked her. Remember that, Buster? Remember how she used to give us kids money?"

It was a good afternoon. We drank tea and ate doughnuts and left on the plate for Shirley the rest of the magical peanut butter cookies that my mother had made especially for her. She showed us the gallon jars of swamp tea that Joe Washington had sent down from Mozhay for her to drink, just a little bit at a time, all day. She was feeling a lot better, she said, felt like she had more energy. She felt cold sometimes, though.

"You should see my X-ray. My lungs, there's all these little silver spots. You wouldn't believe there could be so many. The doctor says that's the cancer, those little silver spots on the X-ray; you should see all of them! Like a swarm of fireflies, it reminds me! But that swamp tea, it's making me feel a lot better. The doctor said that's good, that it makes me feel better. He told me to drink all I want."

"Hey, I ever tell you about when my mother was in the hospital, before she died? I was there all the time, every day, and she knew me even when she didn't know anybody else. Well, she couldn't swallow anymore, you know how that happens? So, they were feeding her through this little tube, and she was saying to me how she would sure like to have a beer. She couldn't drink anything, though, through her mouth; everything had to go in through the tube, and so when the doctor came by I asked him about it. 'She's wishing for a beer'—I told him this privately 'do you think it would be all right if I just poured a little bit of beer in that little tube?' He said to me, 'Shirley, that dear lady can have anything she wants.' That's just what he said, that dear lady could have anything she wanted. So

I brought in a can of beer, and she could watch me pour a little bit into the tube, and she would say, 'Keep it coming, daughter, dear.' Oh, she was funny. 'Keep it coming, daughter, dear.' That's her picture right here, see?" She lifted a handful of photographs from the table. "In this one she's an old lady, but here she's younger than I am now. And in this one, you can just barely see her looking over the railing; she's this little girl right here, just a little girl, at Indian school."

She had put on a sweater and was rocking slowly in the recliner. "I have something for you, Artense. Go in my bedroom, sweetheart; it's past the kitchen, way down at the end of that long hallway, past the bathroom; go in there, and go around the other side of the bed, and underneath the dressing table there's a pair of boots for you. They'll fit you; your feet are small, like mine. You can wear them to dance in; they'll go nice with your dress. You still dance in your blue dress with the red ribbon, don't you?"

Her bedroom was feminine, and more light and tidy than I would have thought. Her bed was made, the pink wallpaper print comforter fluffed up and even around the edges. The window shades were pulled up exactly to halfway; over them, the white lace curtains looked starched, spotless. Her many bottles of colognes and lotions looked attractively arranged on the mirrored tray on the vanity; did she do that deliberately, or did the pattern just occur? The air in the room was dry and smelled like Jean Naté talcum powder; there wasn't a speck of dust anywhere. I found myself tiptoeing into the room toward the tray of perfume bottles, wanting to pick them up and touch them, like a curious little girl on an errand into her grown-up aunt's bedroom. I remembered Shirley at Aunt Lisette's kitchen table, setting her hair in pin curls. In front of her were two glasses of beer. She drank from one, dipped the comb into the other to dampen each lock before she twirled it quickly around her finger and bobby-pinned it against her scalp. I stood at the corner of the table, between my mother and Aunt Shirley, listening to their grown-up lady talk and aching for the day I would be sitting there, too, setting my hair with beer and carelessly enjoying adult freedoms. They could wear whatever they wanted, go to bed at whatever time they wanted. Talk about the color they would paint the kitchen someday and the girl down the street who sat outside in her swimming suit. Buy powder and lipstick at Woolworth. Shirley, who longed for a daughter and never did get one, saw the naked longing on my face and pulled me close to her knees. She picked up the comb to set my bangs into pin curls.

"Here, use water. Buster's not going to want me bringing her home smelling like beer." My mother always set her hair with water.

"Artense's hair's just like mine, so straight it'll never hold the curl if I set it with water. Anyway, the alcohol evaporates when it dries so the smell goes right away; he'll never know it was beer, and her bangs'll keep the set. She'll look just like a teenager, won't you, Artense?"

Facing me from the other side of the bed was a graying and grown-up woman, younger than Aunt Shirley and plainer, without eye makeup or hair rinse. My reflection in the mirror above the vanity raised her eyebrows and smoothed the straight, fine filaments of white hair that sprang from her braids. She didn't touch the perfume bottles.

The boots were behind the pink vinyl footstool that Shirley had pushed into the space under the vanity. They had been brushed and stuffed with tissue paper; the soles were lightly scuffed into circular patterns where the balls of her feet raised and lowered her body nine dips to the left, nine to the right, when she danced. She was taller than I was, and she wore her skirts shorter than I wore mine; the fringe that when she danced swayed and swung from the tops of the boots would be covered by my skirt and barely show as I dipped and pivoted in my restrained version of Shirley's traditional style. When I picked them up, the touch of suede against my fingers was oily and cool, and I shivered, but back in the living room I held them to my heart like a baby and said, "They fit perfect. Miigwech."

"I've been waiting to give them to you. I want you to have them," Aunt Shirley answered. "I've been thinking about you dancing in them."

She didn't live long after that. The small silver spots on her lungs, that swarm of fireflies caught in that mortal pattern in the moment the X-ray was taken, begat, and begat, and begat some more until there finally wasn't enough room for them to move at all. Crowded and static, they turned her lungs into solid sterling, and she died.

The first time I wore them I felt in their leather the outlines of slender, fine-boned feet that weren't mine, and I suppose the boots must have felt in the outlines of my own curved and muscular feet a hesitation, the tentativeness of a new tenant. Her smaller toes had molded subtle scallops not quite the shape of mine into the ends of the gathered vamps; I had to loosen the lacing over the insteps, tighten it at the ankles. At first they felt cool; I stood facing the mirror in the ladies' dressing room watching my cousin Dale Ann comb and braid my hair, and the leather warmed to my body heat and began to yield, relaxing to the shape of my calves and feet. I stood still as Dale Ann scraped my scalp and bent her fingers into gyrating, fantastic shapes that churned out stiff-looking braids that she secured at the ends with abalone buttons, then with a quilled barrette she anchored the white eagle feather and fluff to the tiny braid she had woven across the top of my head.

"How's that?" she asked. "Tight enough?"

"I can't even blink my eyes," I answered, then flexed up and down on the balls of my feet, testing the feel of the boots.

"Are they comfortable on you?" Dale Ann was flexing her own

knees and feet, warming up. Her feet looked chubby in moose hide moccasins that fit tightly as ballet slippers; I could see her high, high insteps undulating under the pink wild roses beaded on the vamps, could see the movement of the tendons working along the sides of her feet and disappearing under her calico leggings, where she kept her hard ankles and sinewy calves under strict, traditional-dancer control.

"I'm working into them." At body temperature, they began to feel like a second skin.

"Where are you ladies from?" The woman next to me in the mirror was gathering the ends of her French braids into a chignon at the back of her neck. The jingles on her red and black dress chinked a silvery scale as she moved her arms.

"Mozhay Point. But we live in Duluth, here," Dale Ann answered. "How about you? Giin i dash?"

"Miskwaa River." She was bent backward from the waist, twisting handfuls of shiny, slippery-looking hair around one fist; as the mass tightened the ends slid apart and out of her fingers and down her back. She laughed, embarrassed. "Oops. I don't usually wear my hair up."

"Here, want me to do that? We have a lot of bobby pins." Dale Ann coiled the woman's hair and wound the coils back and forth into a tight figure eight. Into the middle of the chignon she skewered a beaded hair tie of red sweethearts and black cut glass bugles. "Pretty," she mumbled, with her mouth full of hairpins. "There, that's gonna hold. Too tight?"

The jingle-dress dancer worked her mouth a little and smiled. "No, no, it's all right. I can still move my face."

We laughed.

"Miigwech." She hesitated. "Do you think this skirt is too short? I borrowed my cousin's dress."

"Not really." Dale Ann sounded doubtful.

"It's really nice." I meant that, it was, but the bottom of the jingles brushed the top of the leggings, and once she moved her knees would show flashes of skin while she danced.

I asked her, "Do you have a half-slip on?" I knew she did; I had seen it when she was getting dressed. "You want to trade? Mine is black, and it's longer than yours. It would look like your dress. Nobody would know."

We switched undies, giggling. She said, "My name's Inez."

"I'm Artense. And this is Dale Ann; we're cousins. Hey, that looks good, and the jingles really show against that black. Ready to go out and dance? My daughters are already out there lining up."

"Yeah, let's maajaa." We left the dressing room and walked toward the grand entry lineup at the far end of the powwow circle.

"You gotta be careful out there with us, though," Dale Ann warned. "Sometimes we kick up all these divots and you've got to look out so you don't fall in the holes they leave!" She held on to my arm so she wouldn't fall down laughing.

"Oh, was that you, then, who I noticed doing that up at the Mozhay Point spring powwow? You were dancing so fast it was just dusty out there, you were just a blur, so I couldn't see who it was!"

We quieted down as grand entry time got closer and approached the group of dancers lining up to go into the powwow circle. The flag bearers stood at the front, four men abreast, one with the American flag, one with the Canadian, one with the Eagle Staff, one with the black POW MIA flag. Next were the male dancers: traditionals, some in black velvet beaded with flowers and vines, some in leather and calico; fancy dancers in double bustles; grass dancers, whose shoulders stayed level while their feet and yarn fringes brushed the ground, spun and skipped. Ahead of us, the ladies in buckskin dresses held out their hands for the pinch of tobacco that would be placed in their palms as they entered. Dale

Ann and I lined up behind them, Dale Ann after me because she was younger, then my daughters behind us. Inez from Miskwa River hugged us; she would enter farther down the line, with the jingle-dress dancers.

"Nice to meet you ladies. See you later. Miigwech for helping me. Hey, Artense, I really like your boots; they look good with your outfit."

"They're a gift from my aunt. Miigwech. Nice to meet you, too, Inez. See you out there, then."

Shirley's dance boots entered the powwow circle with my careful steps, matching my toe-heel gliding dip to the beat of the Tamarack Boys' drum's opening song and following the fur-topped moccasins of the graceful elderly lady ahead of me in line, who followed the ladies in buckskin dresses ahead of her, all of us matching our rhythm, left-toe-left-foot, right-toe-right-foot. I always thought that woman traditional dancers looked like a flock of wild geese ready to leave the ground and fly, in that V formation, but of course, because we were traditional dancers and bound by choice to the earth, our feet always touched the ground. We held our tobacco in our left hands, which are closer to the heart than the right; with our right hands we held our fans. Behind us we could hear the jingle-dress lady dancers enter the circle with their singing dresses; rounding the circle, we passed at the entrance the fancy shawl dancers, young women who sprang like deer and spun like dandelion fluff, in colors of the summer sky, and pink and orange sunsets, and the yellow of buttercups and bees. With the entrance of the little children behind the fancy shawl dancers, the line of dancers more than completed a circle. The lead buckskin lady danced the traditional women dancers past the flags and off to the side, where we completed the grand entry song in a line of swaying and pivoting dancing in place, ladies in buckskin or beaded velvet or beribboned calico, all with our feet on the ground and turning as though connected to the same lathe, counting toe-heel in place, four to the left, four to the right, center, four to the right, four to the left.

And now it is this moment, another of the many so unexpectedly profound that they turn instantly tangible, another moment that I learn by rote and remember by heart. To Dale Ann's and my right, my grown daughters, Anjeni and Michelle, have taken their places in that line of women who anchor the powwow, as the women before us, our grandmothers and aunts and older sisters and cousins, anchored the powwow before we became traditional dancers ourselves. I glance at our feet—Anjeni's in gold deer hide with beaded vamps, Michelle's in tennis shoes, mine in Shirley's suede boots—then at our dresses—Anjeni's black sprigged calico, Michelle's black velvet skirt with beaded red, pink, and yellow flowers blooming from dark green vines, my dark blue dress with red ribbon sent to me by Shirley in a dream. As we pivot to the right I see Stan, who holds his hat over his heart with his right hand and holds the hand of our grandson with his left. Mitchell, our grandson, stares at his mother, stunned by her beauty, looking so different from the young woman in jeans and a sweatshirt who went into the women's dressing room. Stan stares at me in the same way. Against the sole of my left foot, where it curves, under the arch, I feel the small bit of tobacco and sage that I placed inside my stocking before I put on the suede dance boots.

I raise my eagle feather to bless and honor them all and include in my dancing prayer my thanks to the Creator for these people I love. And for the ones I will to come to love. And for the ones who have left whom I have loved and love still. And for Aunt Shirley and her boots.

You're welcome, says the Creator.

I wink at Stan, who points with his lower lip to Mitchell, whose shoulders and feet are moving with the song.

THREE SEASONS

BIBOON: MAGGIE IN WINTER

When Maggie fled her family home on the Mozhay Point Indian Reservation headed for the railroad tracks that led to Duluth, it was without her husband, who was because of her lying unconscious on the floor next to the woodstove, or her three oldest children, who in the fall had been blown from home by the winds of seasonal change and federal Indian policy to boarding school. She did take her two small boys and—tied into a flowered quilt—some children's clothing, several potatoes, and a pan of lugallette. And his rifle, which she wrapped in a gunnysack and slung on her back, like an infant. Then she left him, that bastard she hit over the head with the frying pan after he had passed out, unconscious but breathing, on the floor of the two-room tarpapered house that had been her grandma's, on the forty-acre land allotment in Sweetgrass Township that had been taken from that renegade devil-Indian Joe Muskrat and assigned to the LaForce family when Maggie was a little girl.

Andre, that bastard. She had just come in the door with an armful of wood, which stuck to her shawl. When she set the wood down on the floor, it left bits of snow and bark against the plaid wool crossed over her chest. Giizis and Biikwaastigwaan were asleep at the bottom of the bed, their hair stuck to their heads in that damp sleep sweat, from that hard work that children do in their dreams, Giizis snoring and Biik so still in his labor that she placed a hand on his chest to ease for a second her endless worrying that those two, the littlest, her last, would leave, too, in the relentless gusty wake of the three before them. "Biik? Ginibaa?" He breathed. Ah. And she smoothed the quilt over their bodies, faded maroon and pink flowers against a summer sky fogging and running after years of wear and washing to snow and sleet, her wedding quilt. Sixteen irregular large pieces of ladies' dresses crazy-stitched together.

Her wedding quilt. Remember that day. Andre, good-looking little man he was, with those short bowed legs that she couldn't help but follow the first time she saw him walk past her. But he was mean to her when he drank. She knew everybody could see that but nobody said anything, and she was as big as he was anyway and should be able to take care of herself. And Sonny was there too, not showing yet, him, a tiny boy carried right inside Maggie and nobody knew except Andre, not even the priest, so she committed mortal sin going to confession and leaving that out, and right before the sacrament of marriage, too. She supposed her mother knew, the way she was looking at her. Mother had made that quilt in a real hurry, stitched the top together in two days and batted, tied, and finished in two more, pieced so large that sleeves and bodices could be clearly seen clutching and elbowing expanses of skirt. When it was spread on the bed, the quilt told a hundred stories about Mother and Nokom and the aunts and the ladies who had donated whatever they could spare that was suitable for a wedding quilt that needed to be finished quickly.

He pushed open the door and leaned on the frame, Andre, right after she set the wood down, and told her to move her big old hind end and get him something to eat. She put the frying pan on the woodstove, put some lard in to melt, started cutting up the potatoes, and said, "Go wash up, you. Where you been? You stink like Old Man Dommage's place." Next thing she knew, he had her by the hair and he was gasping and wheezing with the work it was to swing her around, and she could smell his breath—bad enough to make her sick—snoose and meat and rotgut wet on her face asking, "Where the hell's Louis?" In their embrace, her mouth so close to his ear she whispered hoarsely, "Hold on, hold on. The supper's gonna burn." He let go and stood there swaying, head down but eyes up staring without focus, putting a lot of work into trying to watch her cook till his legs gave out and he slept on the floor. "Bastard," she thought. Andre, you bastard.

And Maggie realized that she was ready. She scraped the potatoes into the empty lard bucket and set the frying pan on the table, in the center, exactly on the blackened circle that it had charred into the wood that time he grabbed her around the waist and spun her away from the stove so quickly that she hadn't had time to let go of the frying pan and so held it with both hands while she twirled, arcing it high in the air to miss Biik's and Giizis's heads, before she dropped it on the table, where it gonged like a church bell before she went down like a sack of apples.

Ready. She had practiced this so many times in her head that her body moved and her hands did the work without thought. She watched herself do this. First the frying pan, to keep him out for a while. Then the twine. It was under the bed with Andre's broken traps and the lard can that Giizis and Biik peed in when it was too cold and dark for them to go outside. She tied Andre's hands to the biggest trap and then wound the twine around his ankles, his knees, around his shoulders and arms, tying the knot right over where he had torn that hole in the back of his red-and-black buffalo plaid jacket, catching it on the saw next to the woodpile that time he swung at her and missed when she was chopping wood. Then she took the quilt off the bed and wrapped the potatoes, the pan of lugallette, and Giizis's and Biik's other shirts. She woke the boys and helped them put on their shoes and coats and hoods and the mittens she'd made them from the tops of Andre's old socks. Finally, she grabbed the rifle and slung it with the quilt bundle over her shoulder. The boys followed her out the door and down the road all the way to the tracks where the railroad men kept their handcar. She hefted and loaded onto the platform her little boys and the quilt that held what she needed now instead of the hopes and dreams she'd been silly enough to fill it with when she'd married that bastard. Then Maggie stepped up, lifted one end of the pump, and began to move her little boys and her wedding quilt down the tracks to Mesabi, where she hocked the rifle and bought a train ticket to Duluth.

GIIWE-BIBOON: MAGGIE AND HENEN IN LATE WINTER

Henen was a good sister, Maggie'd always thought, a truly good person who would do anything for you, and one of those people everybody liked. When they were girls at mission school, those long years away from home, Henen always got along well with the nuns, was always there at the front of the line all neat and clean when it was time for morning Mass, always spoke up nice and clear just the way they liked, *yes sister no sister please sister thank you sister*, and always pronounced her name just the way the nuns liked it, *Hell-en*. She was the only one of the girls who got to help the sisters make the little communion hosts, and once in a while she put some that got overbaked into her apron pocket and gave them to Maggie and the other girls to eat when they were getting ready for bed. And the nuns never said anything, even though it wasn't allowed, when on those nights when Maggie was so lonesome for Mother that she couldn't get warm she crept down the dark hallway after lights out, between the little girls' and big girls' dormitory rooms, on bare cold feet over icy floorboards that creaked under her weight, to crawl under the covers with Henen.

Henen had taken good care of Maggie all right, and after Henen was sent home after disgracing herself, she began writing to Maggie, her letters so interesting that they would have made good school essays, her handwriting so precise and clean that if she hadn't been sent away they would have been put up on the wall in continuity of that rebuke of the other girls' laziness, sloppiness, and general inability to measure up to the standard set by the nuns' favorite pupil. Maggie read the letters to the other girls in the dormitory; Henen's letters were better than the books from the library shelf. The letters eased and aggravated the girls' homesickness with stories about maple sugaring and picking berries and washing clothes and hauling wood, all in the company of Mother and Baba, Nokom, and all the neighbors at Mozhay Point. Henen didn't mention anything about the baby, or if she did, the letter never got to Maggie. When Maggie got home the next summer, Mother told her not to talk about it to Henen. And Henen didn't say a word about it; the first thing she did when she saw Maggie was give her a new blouse that she had made for her, yellow flowers on white, that sack style that all the grown-up ladies wore, and to say, tell me about all the girls at school, what did you read, are you learning how to embroider, do you want to practice penmanship with me. That was all, no word about a baby, just Henen all cheerful and happy during daylight, fading to silence when the sun went down.

She never did get back to school, Henen. When Sister Rock noticed her belly, that hard round lump below the waistband of her skirt, grown to the size of a small saucepan and pushing her waistband up closer every day to her bust, she confined Henen to the infirmary, where she couldn't be seen by the other girls, to wait for the doctor to arrive and confirm the result of Henen's sin. That evening, Maggie complained of an earache, and in the middle of the night woke Sister Rock by crying in her sleep. The drainage of blood and fluid had soaked through the pillowcase and smeared the sheets and the sleeves of her nightgown. Sister clicked her tongue and muttered, stripped the bed and Maggie, bundled the dirty linens under her arm, and led Maggie out of the little girls' dormitory, down the stairs to the basement, where she threw the wad onto the pile of whites to be washed, then back upstairs. Naked, Maggie shivered in the cold night air of the damp hallways. She crouched as she walked on tiptoe, mortified, in the wake of Sister Rock's large backside, which bounced back and forth under a wool dressing gown the shape and style of her daytime habit, into the infirmary, where Henen sat up in bed and asked, "Wegonen? Nishimay, Maggie, gidaakoz ina?"

Sister Rock shushed Henen and told her to help Maggie into a clean nightgown and then go directly to the kitchen to wait, and to not say a word, not one word.

In the wash basin was clean water for morning. Henen warmed the wash cloth with her hands before wiping the blood off of Maggie's hair and ear and face and her thin and childlike body and whispered that it was all right. She put a clean towel down over the pillowcase and told Maggie that it would feel soft and warm against her sore ear. Then she went to the kitchen, where she slept on the floor of the pantry, rolled in a blanket left for her by Sister Rock.

The next day, because Maggie was too sick to move out of the infirmary, the doctor examined Henen in the pantry, with Sister Rock present but averting her eyes. The girl obediently removed her bloomers and placed one foot on a stepstool. Astonishingly, the doctor knelt before her and leaned his forehead against her knee. He reached under her skirt and ran a thick and warm hand up the inside of her thigh, then probed inside with two fingers, where, she now understood, the baby had been placed. She stared at the gaslight fixture suspended by a metal chain from the pantry ceiling. Out of the corner of her eye she watched, although she tried not to, the doctor's head gleam with a shiny sweat, and his red face twist unhappily while he grunted, reaching in vain for her virginity.

He withdrew and stood, wiping his hands on a dishtowel. "Spoiled. She has been spoiled," he said to Sister Rock. She shook her head.

"On the table, my dear," he said to Henen. He held her hand as she stepped onto the stool. "Lie down, my dear, on your back." He lifted her skirt and folded it back above her waist; sunlight poured onto her skin. In the humiliation of her exposure on an oilcloth-covered pantry work table, she watched patterns of light dance through tree branches that waved in the wind outside the window, casting thin waves of warmth on her round belly, on her baby. The chain that attached the gas fixture to the ceiling was really three metal cords, she could see, braided and painted brown.

Again, the doctor's face twisted, reddened. He pulled a dishtowel from a shelf to cover Henen from ribs to knees, then used both hands to cup, through threadbare cotton faintly yellowed with food stains bleached by the girls in the laundry room, her belly and then prod in a circle around the small saucepan shape that was a baby. A baby. "Oh, yes . . . oh, yes." He prodded her breasts. "Are they sore?" And again her belly. "Ye-e-es. About halfway there, I would guess. Have you felt quickening? Moving?"

"No," she answered softly, thinking, "but I will."

"Well, you will. Would you like to see this, Sister?"

Sister Rock, eyes on a row of canned goods, shook her head.

The doctor fumbled, searching in his pocket, as he had fumbled under Henen's skirt, and placed a piece of horehound candy wrapped in white paper and a lemon drop fuzzy with pocket lint on the dishtowel. He and Sister Rock left Henen in the pantry to step back into her bloomers.

When she got home, she helped her mother and wrote letters. She read every day, silently in the morning and aloud before bed, from the only book in the house, the Bible. When the Indian agent's wife paid Mother for ironing with a length of yellow calico, Henen cut and sewed a new blouse for Maggie on the new kitchen table—heavy and solid as a sow—that Baba had built right in the house. Sitting there one night, sewing with her delicate and even stitches, listening to Baba and Mother talk while they drank raspberry tea, listening to Nokom sucking on her pipe as she lit it with a coal from the stove, Henen felt a tapping from within her belly, a lurch to the side. She hummed a song of gratitude.

The baby never moved again; instead, it shrank within Henen's belly, imperceptibly from day to day but nevertheless steadily from week to week. She began to reach for her belly when alone in the house, or in the outhouse, or when she forgot to keep her hands from idleness, searching in sickening composure for a small body, cupping her belly and using her fingers to prod a circle around the lump that every time she searched was harder, more dense, as the little body of her baby calcified and shrank to the shape and consistency of a robin's egg, until any appearance of a small saucepan shape that was a baby simply disappeared. And then, after that, every day, the spirit of her baby receded from her own and the others that continued to live, growing more and more distant, until when the children came back from school in June it had joined those other baby spirits who, because they were too small to walk, traveled to the other world on the east wind, which carried them gently in the sky, borne by visions of the Great Ojibwe Migration of long ago. Out of sight, they were mourned by bereft earth-bound mothers like Henen.

Henen had taken good care of her all right, so once Maggie got to Duluth, she walked, carrying Biik and holding Giizis's hand, over to the rooming house where Henen was staying to settle in for a while, and of course Henen didn't ask any questions or say a word about that damn bastard Andre or ask where Louis was; that wasn't her way—she had always been very considerate of other people's feelings. The sisters shared the bed and the little boys slept on the floor, and it was like the old days at the mission school except there were no nuns telling them what to do, and except of course for the changes in Henen. It took a couple of days for Maggie to see that all of Henen's ways were just a little more so than they had been the last time she saw her, and then to realize that for years Henen's ways had been each time she saw her just a little more so, till it became clear that life had boiled down and distilled Henen to an exaggeration and mockery of the mission school girl she had been. She was as always kind and polite, and she still wore the brown scapular that the nuns had given her underneath her clothes right next to her skin, but Maggie could see that her sister's drinking was getting closer to winning the upper hand in its battle with her spirit. She indulged the boys, allowing them to do as they liked, never sharing in their discipline, though that was the way the LaForces and everyone else at Mozhay Point helped in the proper raising of children, yet hissed at Biik to never, never touch her things when he opened the bottle of cologne she kept on the dresser. She insisted that Maggie try on her rouge, stroked Maggie's hair, told her that they would never be apart again, that she would take care of her baby sister forever, then spent some of the rent money on a bottle of wine from the blind pig in the basement of the house next door, which she drank, secretly she thought, in the outhouse in the backyard that they shared with the rest of the boarders. She had begun to step stiffly and speak slowly, her lips slightly pursed and drooping at the corners as she attempted the precision of speech and posture that the nuns used to hold her up as both example and reproach in front of the other girls. Her belly slackened to a paunch as her waist thickened, yet her arms and legs grew thinner. Her face had begun to swell with the miseries of times she disappeared for days, reappearing with a bruised nose, a new clip for her hair, puffy eyes, or without her coat or memory of liquor- and smoke-hazed bar flirtations that changed unexpectedly into arguments, fistfights, torn clothes, and abandonment. Henen, too proud to acknowledge those betrayals and mortifications, returned alone, making her way up the walk and through the door with a grace and dignity oddly enhanced by the landscape of her face. And she didn't say anything; that was her way.

When Maggie found a job at the mattress factory, she used her first paycheck to rent a house and brought her sister, now so fragile and needing Maggie as Maggie had needed her when they were girls, to live with her.

Sonny wrote home once a month, always the same letter.

> Dear Mother,
> I hope that this letter finds you well. I am in good health, and doing well in school.
> Sincerely,
> John Robineau

ZIIGWAN: SONNY AND MICKEY IN SPRING

That time we were carrying the wash out for the girls to hang on the lines, me and my cousin Mickey, who we called Waboos at home, we started talking Indian and laughing; we weren't supposed to do that, to the teachers there I guess it was like we were saying dirty words.

"Giziibiiga-ige makak, it's heavy, hey."

"Nimashkawaa."

"Gimashkawaa like a little girl, ha!"

We stumbled with that big old washtub, each on one side of it, holding on to one of the handles. It was heavy, and we leaned our shoulders away from the tub to balance the weight. Mickey, he was so skinny his over-hall strap come off the one shoulder and dragged down his arm, making it harder to carry his side. Well, we were breathing so hard from the work and laughing we didn't even know McGoun was sneaking up behind us till he says real loud, "Hey! Are you boys talking Sioux?" McGoun, he didn't know one Indian from another and sure wouldn't know we were talking Chippewa. I says to the prefect, "No, sir, we weren't talking Sioux." And then Mickey says right after me, "No, sir, we wouldn't do that." McGoun squints his eyes at us and says, "Well, see that you don't," and left. We started laughing so hard he heard and came back and shoved Mickey, who fell right on the ground, and the washtub tipped over so all that white wash load was right in the mud, and McGoun said, "Look what you boys done now," and unhooked that doubled leather strap off his waist and started hitting Mickey with it. Then he had us carry the washtub back to the laundry building, and we had to wash it ourselves, all that big pile of girls' underwear and nightgowns. We were humiliated to be touching all that stuff and the laundry girls so embarrassed that for once they stopped their giggling and looked away at anything but us.

That night when we were getting ready for bed, I could see Mickey had bruises on his upper arm, four fingertip shaped on the back and one larger, thumb shaped on the front, from where McGoun pulled him, just about lifting him right off the ground, and a couple of welts on his skinny hind end. I whispered to him, "Maajaa daa, Waboos, let's get out of here tonight," and he looked back at me and smiled so big, his snaggly and rotting teeth all crooked and his eyes all happy. "Eya, 'ndaa," he whispered back.

We lay there on our beds across from each other and listened to the other boys fall asleep as the light from the moon came in through the windows in wide stripes that moved across the floor and beds so we could see first Thomas on his back, arms out wide, with one leg sticking out of the covers, then Shigog, who pulled his covers over his head so he looked like a ghost. We heard Wesley snort and mumble,

"C'mere, you," and I was glad he was sleeping because he was so wild. All the time me and Mickey were facing each other in our beds, Mickey laying on his right side, me on my left. After a while, when it was pretty quiet except for breathing sounds, we looked right at each other and I said, "Let's go, Cousin," and Mickey's eyes widened there in the dark, then turned into crooked black triangles as he smiled and stood up. We picked up our uniform pants and jackets folded and laid out for morning at the ends of the beds, and our shoes and socks, and walked just quiet across the dormitory floor to the kitchen, where we tied some bread and apples into a dish towel to carry. Then we walked out the front door, leaving it open so nobody'd hear us pull it shut, and walked behind the barn in our nightshirts. We got dressed and slicked our hair down a little with some water from the trough and walked down the road toward home.

It was a long ways from Harrod to Duluth, and we were on the road for three, four days. We walked, and hitched, and slept in fields the first two nights, and even though we were wearing these soldier-style uniforms so anybody who looked could have guessed where we had come from, only one person, this one farmer who picked us up on the third day, asked us if we were from that Indian school. Since Mickey was so bashful and because I was afraid he'd tell the truth, doing so with that big smile of his, I did the talking for us. "Yes, sir, we were sent for," I said, looking solemn. "We had a death in the family and have to get to Duluth." The farmer said he was sorry to hear that; he was going to Allouez in the morning and could give us a ride almost to Duluth; if we wanted we could stay in his barn that night.

We helped the farmer unload the wagon and cleaned up a little in the chicken coop, then his wife set us a nice place to eat at their kitchen table. Fried chicken—relatives of the ones we had just fed—these ones' parts were all separated into sizzling little legs and wings and breasts and looking mighty tasty there in the frying pan. The wife kept getting up from her chair to put more food on our plates, and because she was a big woman, built a lot like those chickens of hers, her front and behind hit the backs of our chairs and the sideboard as she moved, and she clucked these nice little chicken noises and fussed over us, how sorry she was about our loss and what brave boys we were to travel all by ourselves. In the morning she fed us again, and the farmer dropped us off in Allouez in front of the feed store. We walked the rest of the way to Duluth, more than ten miles to home.

Ma was surprised to see us walk in the door; the last time I'd run, McGoun had called the Duluth police, who had come to the house to tell her, so she knew about it by the time I got there. She said, "Sonny, Waboos, namadabin. Gibakade, na? I'll make some tea." She called out the back door for Giizis and Biik, "Ambe, ambe, look who's here." She fixed us tea and ladled out some soup, and we told her all about our trip and felt like heroes. Mickey wanted to get going to Mozhay to see the LaVirage cousins, so after he'd eaten, she gave him two quarters and packed him some food for the road.

It was when we were going out the front door to send Mickey on his way that we saw the black Ford parked in front of the house and McGoun sitting on the running board having a cigarette. He got up as soon as he saw us come out and grabbed me and Mickey each by an arm. "Mrs. Robineau, I am here to escort these young men back to the Harrod School," he said, in this formal and official way but breathing hard because it must have been hard to talk with Mickey squirming and me pulling the way we were. Giizis and Biik hadn't gotten all the way out the front door, so Ma pushed them back before McGoun saw them. They knew what to do, went into the bedroom and under the bed, behind the quilt. Ma went right up to the prefect and took me by the other arm and said, "Mr. McGoun, Sonny is sixteen now and we need him at home, here, to go to work. You can't keep him anymore." It was McGoun's job to bring two boys back, but I have to hand it to Ma, she didn't back down this time and he was losing. Finally he said that I was more trouble than I was worth anyway and shoved Mickey into the backseat of the car. Mickey was too big to cry; he smiled just brave with those snaggly teeth and waved at Ma just before they drove away, but then I could see through the back window that his head was down and I could feel it that he wasn't smiling anymore. We went back inside and Ma told Giizis and Biik that they could come out now.

NIIBIN: GEORGE IN SUMMER

Ma was able to send money to school for train tickets home so that when summer started Girlie and me could come home and not be put to work on the truck farm for our room and board. We had a good time at home. Once it got warm out a lot of people would come to visit at Ma's, stopping by to visit and stay a while, people from Mozhay Point and Lost Lake, relatives and friends, the Brules and Gallettes, the Sweets, the Bariboos. They brought their kids and their quilts and food, flour or salt pork or maybe a sack of rice, if they had some left over from last fall. We had some good times. All day we would be visiting, kids playing and the grownups having tea while they talked, people coming and going. Some of the men got jobs shoveling grain at the elevators or working in the scrap yard and were able to find places for their families to live here in town, too. So now we knew some people here. Good times. And Ma's house was right in the middle of it when Girlie and me got home that summer.

Some nights after it was dark outside we would have a fire in the backyard, in the pit Sonny had dug, and sit to visit, watching till it burned out. Ma would set potatoes in the fire, close to the outside edge and under the wood, to cook. She picked up the potatoes when they were blackened and done, with her bare hands, and handed them out. Split open, the insides looked so white out there in the dark.

Ma was always very generous with people; she had that reputation. She'd give you the shirt off her back, people said. They always talked that way, like they admired her, but I saw people take advantage of her, too, and she died poor, like a lot of other generous people. Not everybody is like Ma, but she didn't care about that. I remember not long after we got home me and Sonny were sleeping on the front room floor after everybody was asleep, and we could hear these people, some friends of some of our cousins, in the kitchen. They were real quiet in there, with the door to the front room shut, making these rustling noises as they unwrapped food that they'd brought for just themselves. Here they were staying at Ma's, and she made them welcome, and with her good manners offering them whatever she had—and that wasn't much. Before everybody went to bed, they'd finished up the coffee she had on hand and ate more than their share of potatoes, so that there weren't going to be enough for everybody for the next day, but Ma didn't say anything because that wouldn't have been polite. And there they were, eating, in the middle of the night there, all by themselves in the kitchen, and there were me and Sonny in the front room, still hungry, listening to them eat. Paper bags rattling. Chewing. Whispering.

They got up early and left with their garbage so we wouldn't know what they'd been up to. When I told Ma about it she said that was their own business and not ours.

"Why should they get away with that, those bums?" I asked.

"Maybe they think they need it."

"Maybe we think we do, too."

"Not like that, we don't."

And Girlie and Aunt Helen just nodded their heads in that way, saying in those voices that sounded like they were singing together, "Mmmm, hmmm," to let me know that Ma was acting the way a person should.

"It was cookies, and doughnuts, and it smelled like they were eating dried meat, too. Next time they come here we should throw them out, those bums."

"People do what they do for reasons we don't know about. They must need it more than we do."

"E-e-en za," Aunt Helen added, "so I've heard," which made Ma laugh.

Ma lived long enough for me to buy a Buick and take her out driving and visiting when I came home, and she made sure that I took everybody else out who needed a ride, too. And let them borrow money. I bought her things I knew she would like, pretty things, a bowl with red and blue stripes painted on the outside, a statue of a little girl holding a flower, a blue powder box with a music box inside—when she opened the lid she could listen to it play while she powdered her face.

I always worked hard, almost as hard as Ma, but I was somehow able to hang on to more of my money. It wasn't easy; it took some compromises that sometimes I think she didn't understand. But she always stood up for me when anybody called me a stingy-gut.

Like I said, she died poor. Gave it all away. Give you the shirt off her back and died poor, like a lot of other generous people.

NIIBIN: MAGGIE IN SUMMER

With the weather getting warm and people able to travel around easier, the house got pretty full, with somebody there to watch the little boys and keep them company while Maggie and Sonny worked: Girlie and George and sometimes Henen if it was a good day, or some of the cousins from Mozhay, who visited for an afternoon, or a week, or a month. Some nights there were people sleeping all over the place. They brought blankets and sometimes food with them and shared what they had.

Maggie's children slept on quilts that she had sewn during the spring on Sundays, her days off, while she watched Giizis and Biik play and roughhouse with Sonny, of pieces cut from clothing donated to St. Matthew's and discarded by Father Hagen because it was too worn for wear. Sonny and George had quilts patched from pieces of men's pants and jackets, dark wools, Girlie a flower garden of brights and pastels, ladies' skirts and dresses. Sonny and George slept on the front room floor, but Girlie brought her quilt into the bedroom and slept with the little boys on the floor next to Maggie's bed. For the first week after she got home from school she had followed Maggie from room to room, kitchen to front room to bedroom, as she did her work at home, cooking, cleaning, ironing, sewing, and when Maggie sat in the rocking chair, Girlie sat on the floor next to her, touching the hem of her mother's skirt with the back of her hand or pinching it between her thumb and first finger, being Maggie's little girl again for just a little while.

Andre showed up one day while Maggie was at work and made himself at home. When she got home he was lying asleep on the front room floor on the wedding quilt that her mother had made them, the one she took when she left the allotment, that he must have taken off her bed, with his head on his damn jacket, and Girlie was in the kitchen slicing up some pork and lard for when he woke up. "Ai," she thought, "sshhtaa," and was going to say something when Girlie turned from the stove and said with a happy smile, "Look who's here!" Maggie thought, well the children were glad to see him; he was good to the children. Why ruin it for them?

He stayed two days and then took Sonny and George to find a ride with him back up to Mozhay Point; Maggie didn't see them again until the end of summer when the boys walked in the front door swaggering a little because they had cash money from working at the tourist stand and ricing. They had Waboos with them but not their father, whom they'd left up at Old Man Dommage's.

GIIWE-NIIBIN: GIRLIE IN LATE SUMMER

George came back to town from Mozhay with Mickey right before we had to go back to boarding school, which was a good thing because I didn't want to have to go on the train by myself and then have to try to explain to Mr. McGoun where they were. It was going to be hard enough to leave Mama and the little boys, who were really old enough to go to school and really shouldn't be left alone like that when she went to work. Mama was doing everything she could to keep those boys with her and not send them to Indian school, but I knew she was going to have to send them sometime. One night we could hear her and one of the uncles talking out in the front room, late when they thought we were asleep, me and the little boys. The big boys were outside in the backyard by the fire, so it was just Mama and Uncle Noel sitting out there, the rhythm of Ma in the rocking chair making tiny rumbles against the floorboards, once in a while Uncle Noel spitting into a tin can, very soothing it was so I was lulled almost asleep till they started talking about the little boys. Noel was saying how they needed somebody to watch them with Mama having to be at work and he didn't see how anybody else could take them; once Indian school started the older children would be gone; Giizis really had to go to school and who could watch Biik? She couldn't count on Henen to do it; Henen had her own troubles and needed watching herself; maybe Maggie should go home. Grandma was too sick even to leave the allotment for Duluth; she wouldn't be able to take care of them even if Maggie sent them up to Mozhay and stayed in Duluth to work.

"Who else would watch them, my girl?" he asked.

Mama's voice was so quiet I had to hold my breath to hear her. "I don't know, I just don't know," she said.

Biik and Giizis were scared; they pushed closer to me so that their little bodies got my sides all hot and sweaty, Biik's eyes big so he looked like a little owl there in the dark, and Giizis trying so hard not to cry that he shook. Little brothers. I sat up on the floor cross-legged and sat one on each knee to lean back against me while I rocked them side to side. Side to side. Little brothers. I played with Giizis's ears a little because that always made him all lovey and sleepy, and after a while his shoulders stopped that shaking and he turned his round face around up to look at me and smile before he fell asleep.

So it was true what I'd been telling the matron at school, Mama needed me at home. Matron didn't know about Giizis and Biik and I couldn't tell her, so she couldn't really understand, and I suppose she must have thought Mama must have something else going on—maybe she thought Mama was a drinker like Aunt Helen. Matron said she thought that school was a good place for me.

They all drank, of course, all of them, Mama and Aunt Helen and Daddy and Louis and everyone who was old enough to, and when I was home whenever they had a bottle it was the same thing. But I have to tell you that no matter how anybody else acted, Mama and Aunt Helen always acted like ladies, no matter what. They would sit there at the table perched on the edge of their chairs, with their backs straight and their skirts neat and straight over their legs just like they had learned from the sisters when they were at that mission school, and they would just sip, very delicately; they were never guzzlers. Every once in a while they would lean their heads together and laugh or, when they got pretty serious, sit very close together and talk in their low silvery voices, a pair of doves. And ladies, always ladies. Their indirect and kind eyes, behind Mama's lovely and still mask and Aunt Helen's, occasionally slipping when her graciousness was frayed by that betrayal of her spirit, met reality with courage and mission school manners. To this day, and I am an old woman now, two generations past the age they were in the times I am talking about, I sip my liquor, too, and remember how a lady is supposed to act. Pretty old-fashioned for these days, I guess, and because I am the only one left of all Maggie's children, the first daughter and the last to die, Mama's ways and Aunt Helen's, too, that lived their longest in me will probably die with me. And their faces, too; I am the last living person who remembers those composed masks, marked by life to a state beyond beauty, and those kind and indirect eyes.

We didn't want to leave, George and Mickey and me, but like everybody else we didn't have any choice. We would have to get on that train and get off at Harrod and somebody would be there to pick us up in the wagon to make sure we got to school. We would report to the matron and the prefect, who would march us to the girls' and boys' dormitories to get deloused and fumigated and try on our uniforms to see if they still fit. Mickey had gotten so tall that he was going to need a whole new uniform, jacket and pants and shoes, and I guessed that when they saw how big he was they'd take him out of the laundry and put him to work at the truck farm or the carpenter shop. That was the summer that he really grew, though he stayed skinny; his clothes had been big on him last spring but now his wrists stuck out of his shirtsleeves and his over-halls flapped around a couple of inches above his ankles when he walked. I asked him one night when we were watching the fire outside about what happened when McGoun got him back to school last spring. He told me that McGoun gave him a beating with that doubled leather strap, took away his quarters, then put him in the lockup room in the basement for three days. "It was nothin'," he said, McGoun would get his one day. He smiled then, crooked and snaggletoothed, like

Mickey, but with glints and flashes of something hungry and wolfish; in changing from boy to man he was also changing from Waboos to Maingen.

DAGWAAGIN: MAGGIE IN AUTUMN

Giizis's last day as one of the little boys hidden at home was the day that the superintendent of the Indian school himself showed up on Maggie's porch with tribal census records verifying that Vernon Gallette, son of Marguerite LaForce and Louis Gallette, was seven years old, that he lived with his mother, and that he was not attending school. He left a half-fare ticket for Giizis and full-fare tickets for Girlie, George, and Mickey.

The next morning, they walked to the train station, Mickey and George carrying the lunch that Maggie had packed and their box of extra clothes, Girlie holding Vernon's hand. Maggie stayed on the porch, holding Biik and waving his hand, bye-bye. "Take care of your little brother," she called, "see you in the spring," as she watched them walk away, growing smaller and smaller in her sight. Just before they disappeared around the corner, they turned to wave again, George and Girlie smiling to set an example for little Vernon, whose round moonface was shiny and stretched with crying. Waboos waved, then became Maingen, who thought of that day that would come, and smiled with bared pointed teeth, that thin young wolf hungry for the day McGoun would get his.

Maggie kept her smooth and pleasant mask in place until they turned the corner. Her composure slipped for just a moment, exposing ravages of grief that made her look like Aunt Helen's twin, but then she pressed the crook of one arm to her eyes to absorb her tears, which darkened the print of her cotton work dress sleeve, dried, and disappeared. Then, remasked, she smiled at Biik, took his hand and led him back inside, set him down, and knelt to fold her children's quilts, smoothing and soothing the prints of their bodies into squares that she then pushed under the bed. She had practiced this so many times in her head that her body moved and her hands did the work without thought. Without direction from heart or head, her hands washed dishes, swept the floor, washed and dressed Biik, stroked his hair while they waited on the porch for Andre, helped him into Andre's brother's car for the ride up to her brother Earl's house at Mozhay Point, waved bye-bye, see you soon little man, pulled her coat up over her arms and shoulders, pulled the front door shut behind her. Her feet, at their even greater distance than her hands from head and heart walked. Walked to the mattress factory, up the stairs, to the time clock, to her sewing station, where she worked without thought, eyes down, face composed, heart heavy and still as her face and as unreadable, as with the rhythm of the earth she prepared for winter, the season of hibernation and dreams of her children's return.

MAGGIE AND LOUIS, 1914

The first time Maggie saw Louis she was sitting at the work table in the laundry building, next to the window for the light, mending stockings. She sat erect on the wooden chair, her body held inches away from the back in order to demonstrate proper posture to the group of girls learning how to set the darning egg into the curves of toes and heels.

"Watch how I do this, first," she said, demonstrating to the silent row that sat across from her at the table. "Use the darning needle to pick up the ends of knitted weave not torn or frayed, like this, do you see? Then cross it back and forth to the other side of the hole or the worn-out spot, do you see? And then do the same on the other two sides, but this time weave the needle over and under the threads you cross over. Don't bunch up the threads, and don't pull too tight; we want to leave a darn with edges smooth and even so that when the stocking is worn it doesn't rub against the foot or the shoe—that makes the hole come back bigger, and you will have wasted your time." She mended over a frayed heel and held up the stocking. "Do you see?" The girls nodded.

"You may thread your needles and begin." The girls' matron, who would stay with the sewing class until she was sure that Maggie was capable of keeping the group in order, directed the girls in her deep and ringing voice. Maggie distributed a wooden darning egg and several black machine-knitted cotton stockings to each girl. They silently wetted and pinched the ends of threads between their lips, squinted to thread their needles, dropped darning eggs into their stockings, and sat straight as Maggie, their backs inches from the backs of the chairs as they began to mend.

So quiet they were. All she could hear was breathing. One girl snuffled and swallowed; the matron glared. The girl said, "Pardon me, Miss," dragging out the *a* and dropping the *r* in an accent from north of Miskwaa Rapids.

Next to Maggie a heavyset girl with thick, coarse black hair braced her mending against her bosom, her nearsighted eyes wide open and nearly meeting at the bridge of her nose with the effort of trying to see black thread against black stocking. She looked up at Maggie; her pupils slowly uncrossed, focusing. Her smile was dazzling, her mouth a crescent of perfect white teeth, her round face dark-skinned and smooth. "She looks like she must be from Fleur de Pomme," Maggie thought. The matron rapped on the table with her knuckles. "Eyes on your work," she said sternly. The nearsighted girl ducked her head.

Breathing. Some girls breathed lightly, some heavily, through their mouths, concentrating both to obey the matron and to please the new helper, an Indian girl dressed like a white lady, like a teacher. After a while, warm breath, curling ribbons of air, gently waved and wound through the room, twining air tendrils around the girls, around Maggie and the matron, around the work table and chairs, the baskets of mending, the ironing table, the gaslight that hung from the center from the ceiling on a heavy chain. The room became dreamlike, the seamstresses sleepy. Someone's nose whistled softly and plaintively, reminding Maggie of the cries of ducklings swimming behind their mothers at the shore of Lost Lake in late summer, paddling strenuously with infant webbed feet, straining to keep up. "Don't leave me behind, don't leave me behind," their tiny weeping coos begged pitifully. Warm late-summer air wound and curled over the lake, twining damp tendrils around the ducklings and their mother, around Maggie and the rushes that grew higher than her shoulders, around the pale green frieze of ripening wild rice near Muk-kwe-mud Landing, across the lake. Maggie leaned into a crescent of air that supported her as she bent forward from the waist to scoop up and cradle in her hands the last duckling, the smallest and slowest, the one forgotten by its mother and left behind, the duckling that was really a darning egg inside a crumpled long black stocking, and stroked its downy back. "Shh, shh, she'll back soon," she soothed the baby, her lips against its soft feathers.

An adenoidal gasp and snort from the girl with the accent from north of Miskwaa Rapids broke the rhythm of the room; the ribbons of air roiled and snapped, and Maggie jumped, sticking the duckling with the darning needle.

"Pardon me."

"Elizabeth, do you need a drink of water?"

"Thank you, Miss, no," she said, pronouncing the *a* as an *e*.

"Well then, for goodness' sake stop that, or you will have to leave the room."

As the rhythm resumed, Maggie lost her concentration, distracted by Elizabeth's desperate efforts to breathe quietly through her mouth. To cover the distressing stifled gasps, she hummed, stopped, caught the matron's eye. "Can they sing while they work?"

"Yes, that would be fun, wouldn't it? Let's sing. But, before we do, don't forget to sit up straight." The matron clapped her hands twice, for emphasis. The sleepy girls roused.

"Do you know 'Jeanie with the Light Brown Hair'? That's a

pretty song I like." Maggie began to sing. The matron followed in her ringing voice, waving to direct the girls to do the same.

They sang the song over several times, until the girls followed most of the words and the melody. The mood in the room again became dreamlike as Maggie, the matron, and the row of young girls sang wistfully about the lovely and beloved Jeanie, "borne like a vapor on the soft summer air," singing wild notes that were then warbled by blithe birds. Jeanie with the light brown hair, happy as dancing daisies. Their hands and wrists mended stockings gently and gracefully in time to the melody; the needles and black stockings might have been silent violins. Maggie led the girls again to the end of the song, holding, in her voice like a silver flute, "bo-orne li-i-i-ike. . . ."

The matron's voice cracked slightly, and she cleared her throat. Embarrassed, she smoothed the false fringe hairpiece pinned over the top of her head, where the hair had thinned, and adjusted her spectacles, peering and squinting at the girls. "Let's hum it this time," she suggested.

As the silent and industrious violins accompanied the song without words, the old matron swayed and smiled pensively. What was she thinking about? Maggie wondered. A lost love, or a longed-for love? A memory, or a dream? Matron was young, Maggie imagined—her blue eyes were round as a kitten's, her light brown hair a silken puff of pompadour above her smooth white forehead. A duke's daughter, she danced gracefully in the arms of a tall young man—a soldier, perhaps, thought Maggie, who had read and reread every novel in the St. Veronique Mission School library—a commoner, whose feet, in shiny black boots, twirled deft scallops around her ruffled and sweeping skirt. Their love was the more beautiful because it was doomed, denied. Alone and bereft, Matron would live out her life teaching Indian girls to sit up straight, to make their beds with sheets pulled and mitered tightly at the corners, to emulate the bleak motions of her existence. Maggie sighed at the poignancy of Matron's life; the humming girls sighed with her at the poignancy of Stephen Foster's dream of Jeanie with the light brown hair.

With a light tap against the window, a shadow flew across the black wool oval held in the palm of Maggie's left hand, so quickly that she thought a bird must have become confused by the glass and dashed against the window, thinking it was part of the sky. She looked up for the swoop of a wing; instead, a brown gingham shirt appeared to dance momentarily in midair—the sleeves fluttered and waved, the tails lifted, then the shirt half spun and sped away. Black broadcloth, a man's coat, moved into the space and stopped, flapping its sleeves. "McGoun! Robineau! Stop that boy!" The black broadcloth coat moved away from the window and down the stairs toward the yard and the barn. Scarecrowlike in his baggy pants, which rippled in the seat beneath where the wind lifted the pleats of his jacket, the upper-school teacher, Mr. Greeney, continued to shout. "McGoun, where are you? Robineau! Stop that boy!"

The brown plaid grew smaller and smaller as the boy ran toward the brush at the edge of the school grounds, blurring into the dull dusty brown of dried leaves. Except for the color of his hair he might have become lost to the sight of Mr. Greeney and the young Indian man who ran out the barn door in pursuit. The color was his betrayal, a near-black copper that the intensity of the oblique late-day sun lit to a red beacon.

"It's Louis!" one girl whispered.

"Lisette's brother!"

"Is he going run again?"

"He'll get caught, him!"

The matron clapped her hands. "Silence! Young ladies, eyes on your work. We are mending stockings here."

The girls quieted; then the sound of the cook ringing the triangle that hung outside the dining hall created a rustle of dresses and heads turning and whispers, the sound of doves in wind.

The matron clapped twice. "Put your things away." The girls gathered thimbles, needles, thread, and scissors into small cardboard sewing boxes that they placed on a shelf. "Line up." They formed a queue, shortest to tallest, by the door. "March." The smallest girl opened the door and held it as the girls filed out. Each said, "Thank you, Miss" as she left. Then the small girl closed the door and joined the line.

"You did very well, Marguerite. They were following your directions, I think." The matron held several stockings up into the light from the window. "There will always be mending for them to do, of course, but some of the girls, if they show a knack for sewing and get something done, can start cutting out summer-weight dresses for the little ones soon."

"Have they learned to follow a pattern, Matron?"

"Some have; the others will have to learn. Please call me Julia—among the female staff we use first names. With the men we don't, of course."

"Of course."

She would have to call Andre "Mr. Robineau."

"Shall we walk to the dining hall? We use the cook's lavatory to wash before meals." She looked curious. "Is Harrod anything like the Catholic mission school?" she asked, wondering if it was true that the young woman, newly hired to help sew and care for the younger children, had been taught by the religious sisters to speak French and make lace.

"It was smaller, and there were only girls, no boys. And the teachers were Sisters." Sister Cecile might at that very moment be grasping a little girl's arm and leading her to the front doors of the classroom building to kneel on the wooden stairs, on a white navy bean. She might be scolding the little girl, as she had Maggie, lisping through a fine spray of spit, "This is what happens to girls who talk like savages. Next time you'll remember English." Her fingers and thumb might leave light blue-gray prints on the little girl's upper arm, four small circles on the underside, one larger on the outside, that the little girl might press with an index finger as she examined them before putting on her nightgown, just before prayers, feeling and controlling the faint ghost of pain and remembering the grasp of Sister Cecile's strong and holy fingers.

"Did you enjoy your studies?"

"Yes, I did, but I enjoyed sewing the most." Her sister, Henen, had been the better student, and the Sisters' favorite; if she had been white, she might have become a Sister herself. Henen stood up straight, kept her fingernails clean, and enunciated carefully, copying Sister Jean Baptiste—'Mar-geh-reet. Hell-en. Par-don me. Good mor-ning." She read aloud without stumbling. Her mathematics problems were solved correctly and written neatly. Her lacemaking was exquisite. Her handwriting samples, disciplined Palmer Method arabesques and curlicues that matched the lace she made, were exhibited on the wall for the Indian agent to see when he visited the school. So delicate and refined was her touch that she was excused from kitchen work to assist Sister Therese with the preparation of the communion hosts before they were consecrated. At morning Mass she knelt without fidgeting while she prayed; at the altar railing she concentrated on the gift of the Eucharist with beseeching eyes, which closed in prayer as the priest placed the host on her tongue.

"Why can't you be more like Helen?" Sister Cecile asked the girls, nearly every day. The girls looked away from the paragon in sympathy; it was mortifying to Henen, of course.

They were, actually, more like Henen than Sister Cecile knew; or, Henen was more like them than Sister Cecile knew: before being sent to the mission school, Henen had, more than Maggie, absorbed all that had been taught at home by a baptized mother and old-fashioned, traditional grandmother—to be thrifty, industrious, helpful to others, modest, reserved and soft-spoken—virtues that she practiced so overtly that the nuns didn't feel the need to watch her closely and never heard that she talked in Ojibwe language to the younger girls while she braided their hair in the morning or helped them to keep their clothing neat and their shoes clean and their sums and letters lined up in rows as neat as the two columns the girls made to march from the dormitory to morning Mass. The girls could see that Henen had been raised properly at home: she had been kind and generous, respectful and humble, concerned with the other girls' well-being. Left at home, she might have become knowledgeable about healing and herbs or about the old sacred stories that grandparents told during the dark winter months. She might have learned the old ways by heart and might have chosen and taught others to do the same when she became an old woman, the venerable grandmother of a large clan family. Instead, Sister Cecile thought that Henen would make a fine mother's helper, perhaps for a wealthy family in Duluth or Minneapolis, when she finished school.

It was quite a shock to everyone, but especially the Sisters, when Henen was sent home from the mission school in disgrace.

"I hope that you will enjoy working at Harrod," said the matron. "There is a great deal to be done here, and as you have probably guessed, some of the students, the boys in particular but some of the girls, too, are quite wayward. Not completely their fault, of course; their families are so backward. So unfortunate. It is our task to correct what we can."

The walkway between the classroom building and dining hall was wide enough for only two people, and so the three males who approached from the opposite direction stepped off of the concrete to allow the ladies to pass. One man removed his hat; the other looked quickly at Maggie, then at the sky. Each held an upper arm of the boy in the brown gingham shirt, which was open and missing its buttons. The skin of one shoulder showed at the seam, where a sleeve had been torn nearly off.

The larger man nodded courteously at the women. "Miss Hall. Miss LaForce. We got him. He didn't get very far this time."

The matron shook her head. "Tsk tsk. What a shame. What a lot of trouble it is to have to spend time on this, Mr. McGoun."

"It is. We are on our way to the laundry. It will be solitary tonight for this boy. Once again."

"Miss LaForce," the matron asked, "have you met Mr. Andre Robineau? He works in the barn and helps with handyman duties, but as you can see all of the staff must take care of other situations as they arise."

"Yes, we have met." The matron must not have realized that they were both from Mozhay Point, Maggie thought. Of course, everyone from Mozhay knew Andre Robineau. He was the handsomest man on the entire reservation, the handsomest man she had ever seen.

Andre tipped his cap and looked Maggie directly in the eye, like a white man; she felt flustered. "Good evening, Miss LaForce." He had gone to Harrod since he was six years old and stayed to work after he finished the fifth grade, at seventeen. He knew the proper way to address a young woman who worked for the school, Indian or white.

During the exchange, the captive boy in the brown gingham shirt waited courteously, as if he were on a stroll with two friends, as though the men beside him weren't each gripping one of his arms. As though his hair weren't a sweat-stiffened mass of dark-red flames. As though his shirt weren't torn, his breathing weren't exhausted and ragged, as though there weren't welts rising on his exposed shoulder. His eyes were clear and calm; above all, they were patient. "Don't feel sorry for me," they said to Maggie. "It doesn't hurt at all. It's nothing to me at all. I don't even notice. There is more to life than this."

She didn't see Andre in the dining hall. Maggie helped the matron oversee the children's table manners; he stayed in the kitchen to do the cook's lifting and carrying. The children ate quickly and neatly—not a drop of milk or single baked bean or potato lump or slice of carrot or crumb of bread was left on the tables. Each child waited silently for the others to finish, hands folded neatly on the edge of the table, then when the matron clapped her hands, two children from each table of twelve collected the plates, spoons, and mugs and brought them to the kitchen. When she clapped again, the children stood and pushed the long benches under the tables. When she clapped for the third time, they marched out the door in line, table by table. After the children left, the matron and Maggie filled plates and carried them into the small teachers' dining room off the kitchen. They sat at the cold end of the table, near the drafty outside door, below the teachers, who had finished their own dinners and were drinking coffee.

Andre backed through the swinging door from the kitchen with a tin plate in one hand and a tin cup in the other. He placed them on the table. "For the solitary room."

"When you have quite finished, Maggie, will you take Louis Gallette his dinner?" The matron had removed her shoes and was cooling and resting her feet on the wooden chair across the table. In the chair next to them, Maggie tried to ignore, while she ate, the fetid raisin-and-onion scent that rose from them and mingled unpleasantly with the aroma of the beans and potatoes on her plate. Inhaling through her mouth and exhaling through her nose she had nearly bolted the food, which pressed in an unpleasant lump just below the base of her throat.

"Yes, I can do that now, Miss."

"Julia," said the matron, wiggling her freed and airing toes.

Maggie listened to the matron's instructions courteously, keeping the expression on her face smooth and pleasant. She had seen similar instructions carried out when the "recalcitrants"—disobedient girls at the mission school—were disciplined.

Outside the laundry building, she opened the slanting cellar doors to the basement and swung them as far as they would go on their hinges, leaving them resting wide open to light the stairway, which was dark and smelled of lye soap and mildew. The wooden steps felt cold and soft through the thin leather of her soles. When she opened the door at the bottom of the stairs, the carbolic mustiness that had been growing and expanding within the heat and confines of the basement hit her face like a damp rag thrust over her nose and mouth. "Huh," she breathed to expel the smell, and was answered by a gasp and huff from the dark and empty hallway. Fighting the impulse to run, she asked, "Is someone there?" The hallway huffed again. Her eyes adjusted to the near dark, and she saw the coal-fired water heater at the end of the hall, sucking in wet lye and mildew air, which it expelled with a huff into the rusty cylinder below the cistern of heating water. The gaslight in the middle of the hallway, turned low, provided just enough light for her to see the two doors that Julia had told her to look for. The one to the coal bin was solid; a square had been cut into the top half of the other, the door into the solitary room, and was covered by wood strips nailed to the outside that created a latticed grill, rougher than but similar to the window into a confessional. "Bless me, Father, for I have sinned," Maggie thought.

A boy's unchanged voice, mild and sweet, answered from behind the grill, "Yes, Miss."

Louis stood with his face pressed to the grate when he heard the cellar doors being swung open and leaned against their hinges. Supper, he thought. He had been there before and so knew that it would come after the other children and the teachers had eaten, brought by Mr. McGoun, Mr. Robineau, or the matron on a tin plate, and that there would be smaller portions of food, not enough to fill his stomach, as part of his punishment.

The second time that he saw Maggie was through the wooden grate of the solitary room door, and every time he remembered it he pictured the shaded outline of a young woman against the twilight let into the cellar of the laundry building by an opened doorway. The shadow bent to pick up a tin plate and cup from the ground that she had set them on and walked cautiously down the cellar steps. At the bottom of the stairs she placed the cup into the crook of her other elbow and opened the door with her freed hand.

He heard steps, light on the basement stairs, then the doorknob turning. The steps into the basement were hesitant, brushing the concrete with a soft, gritty-sounding scrape. It's not Mr. Robineau, he thought. Not McGoun.

She walked from the dark end of the basement into half-light, a motion of cotton shirtwaist that captured yellow stripes against brown from the gaslight in the middle of the basement ceiling. Through the grate he saw her, then, in partial images that appeared, disappeared, and reappeared rapidly through squares of wooden strips. Woman, he saw, carrying a tray of food. She turned toward the door. Dark hair in a knot on the back of her neck. That Indian woman, the one he'd seen walking with the matron. Strong-looking, tall as Mr. Robineau. She was looking around, trying to peer into the corners. She sighed, hummed under her breath. She ducked nervously to look under the slate tub. She cleared her throat, swallowed. "Is someone there?" she asked. Her voice was soft, a near whisper.

"Yes, Miss," he answered from behind the grill.

Punishment. The first time he ran away was the day after he arrived at Harrod from Grand Bois. He waited until bedtime, when the boys were undressing and putting on their nightshirts. The night before, he had laughed at the sight of boys' heads above those long white dresses that looked like women's underwear.

"Mindemooye," he had said to the boy in the next bed. "Old woman, gonna put on your nightgown?"

"Nightshirt. It's a shirt."

"Gawiin, it's a dress! You look like a mindemooye!"

"Mindemooye, giin!" the other boy laughed and pushed Louis in the chest. "Old lady, yourself!"

Louis balled up his nightshirt and tossed it at the other boy. "Here! Bring it home to your grandma!"

The prefect had tapped them both on the head with the doubled leather strap he carried. "No horsing around. Talk English. Get undressed and get into bed."

The boys slept on their backs with hands at their sides above the blankets. "We look like a bunch of dead people laid out," thought Louis. "I ain't staying here."

The second night he approached the prefect while the boys were undressing. "I have to go outside," he said.

"Nobody goes outside. Get ready for bed."

"Have to." He walked toward the door.

The prefect grabbed him by the back of the shirt. "What do you think you're doing?"

The boy from the bed next to Louis's explained. "Where he comes from, they mean the toilet. He don't really mean outside, he means the toilet."

"Is he stupid? He knows the toilet is down the hall."

"He just means the toilet; he's mixed up because they always say 'outside' when they mean they have to do their business at Grand Bois, and that's where he comes from."

"Do you mean the toilet?" the prefect asked.

Louis nodded.

"Well, from now on, say so."

Louis had walked out of the dormitory room and down the hall toward the toilet, moving more quickly and quietly as he passed the door, and then sprinted down the stairway and out the front door, where he was caught by Mr. McGoun, who wrapped one heavy arm around Louis's skinny waist and the other around his skinny neck and half-carried the boy, who struggled like a cat, to the solitary room in the basement of the laundry building, where he spent only one night, because it was his first offense.

His mother's family, the Eberts, were known for their patience; his father's, the Gallettes, for their ability to endure discomfort, even hardship, without complaining. Louis bore each confinement, beating, and deprivation of food with calm, dry eyes and watched and waited for the next opportunity to escape.

"Are you hungry? I have brought your supper." He watched Maggie, through a series of strips and squares, set the plate and cup on the floor. "How does the door open?"

He told her where the key to the padlock was kept, how it needed to be pushed deeply into the keyhole and forced to the right.

She tried it several times, thinking, "What if the laundry building caught fire? The boy would die." On the fourth try, the side of her index finger caught on the padlock as it clicked open. She wound her handkerchief quickly over the bleeding finger and opened the door. The boy blinked in the half-light.

"You must sit on the bed." Orders from the matron. "I will put your food on the chair."

"I can carry it in for you. Did you hurt your hand?"

Louis stepped outside the cell, which was strictly forbidden, Maggie knew; she stepped inside. She saw a cot with a dirty mattress and a moth-eaten, linty blanket, a wooden kitchen chair, and in the corner a chipped and rusting chamber pot. It was so dark, the smell so foul. She turned back to the doorway, to the boy whose dirty, dark-red hair gleamed like feathers under the gaslight. "Just a moment, I will tidy this." Would he run? "Wiisinin," she said, to comfort him. "Eat your supper."

He had intended, once he maneuvered her into the cell, to push past her and run up the stairs and out of the building. It was nearly dark; she didn't know where McGoun would be. She did not look as though she would want to scream. She would have to try to find McGoun, to find help. This would take time; he would have a good start. By morning he could be nearly halfway to Duluth; by night he could be in a boxcar, on his way home to Grand Bois.

"Gii bakade, ina?" she asked. "Are you hungry?" In English, her soft voice had a slight accent; in Ojibwe, an inflection of home. "Namadabin. Wiisinin."

He didn't run. He sat on the floor and ate, watched her bend to pick up the chamber pot and carry it to the slate tub next to the furnace, where she poured out the urine and then rinsed the pot with water from the cistern. She carried it back into the cell and came out with the blanket, which she brought up the cellar stairs. Seated on the basement floor, outside the cell door, he heard the dull flap of the blanket being shaken in the night air, of a woman's hand swatting dust out of woven wool. He watched her walk back down the stairs. Her feet, he saw, were small; her shoes were ladies' boots, like a teacher's, with high heels, laced severely at slender ankles.

"Will you help me turn the mattress?"

The cell was so small that the young woman and boy had to carry the mattress out into the basement in order to turn it. Under gaslight, the stains took on brilliant incandescent colors: blood was maroon and pink, urine sepia and mustard. He turned his head, ashamed, wanting to lie, to tell her that he had not caused this, to spare them both the embarrassment.

The other side of the mattress was as stained, but in duller hues, and she thought it felt dryer.

"This will be more comfortable, I think."

He nodded. Should he run? In the near darkness of the cell, her white shirtwaist absorbed most of the yellow gaslight. She looked so clean, he thought, to be in that bad place, to be touching the filthy mattress. He had looked at her fingernails, which were short and immaculate, had accidentally brushed her hand, which felt so smooth and dry against the gritty sweatiness of his own.

"I will take the plate and cup. Will you be going to sleep, now?" She was standing beside him, under the gaslight. A strand of hair had come loose from the knot with the work of carrying and turning the mattress and hung at the side of her face, curving in an s shape around her cheekbone and down to her jaw. She bent her head to that side, pulled a hairpin from the knot, and held it between her teeth while she tucked the strand back into the knot. Her teeth looked as clean as her shirtwaist, he thought; her mouth, which she closed as she pulled the hairpin from between her teeth, gentle and kindly.

"Thank you, Miss." Louis answered. "Mino pagwad. The food was good." He re-entered the cell and lay on the mattress. She covered him with the blanket and closed the door.

He saw her again, through the grate, in a series of strips and squares under the gaslight. "When you shut the padlock, you need to push it together hard, or it won't stay locked," he told her. "Don't cut yourself again."

The mattress and blanket smelled of night air, almost like sleeping outside, he told himself. He closed his eyes and imagined stars, a half-moon, and, just as he fell asleep, the northern lights arcing and bowing in waves of green, blue, and purple. One of them became Miss LaForce, who gracefully bent into the crescent of air that supported her to place a plate and cup on a cloud, then shook a damp wool blanket into the cold night sky, loosening bits of lint that crystallized into a spray of ice that fell to the earth, green and purple and blue crystals blowing and drifting outside the cellar door, filling in the footprints that Miss LaForce's shoes had made in the freezing mud. In his sleep, Louis heard the sound of ice falling on ice. He rose and floated through the grate, in strips and squares that became his whole and solid self standing on the basement floor. He walked up the stairs and touched the slanting cellar doors, which opened like a pair of wings. Above his head the northern lights grew larger and stomped mightily in the sky around Miss LaForce, whose pointed lady shoes kneaded a cloud, toes-heels, toes-heels, Miss LaForce, who pivoted slowly in the sky, her brilliant shawl rising and falling over her broad shoulders and bent elbows, like the wings of a dragonfly.

"Ambe niimiwin, come and dance," came the invitation from the sky. "Ambe nagamon, come and sing."

"Waas noodin, shining wind," he acknowledged, inhaling cold, icy air, which cleared his lungs and opened his eyes. Humming, with his eyes on the lights, he danced into Maggie's footprints.

REFUGEES LIVING
AND DYING IN THE WEST
END OF DULUTH

We wouldn't be back at Aunt Babe's house until two years later, the afternoon in 1970 after Louis's funeral, which would be in most ways but not all a different type of gathering. After the funeral, the dining room would look bare, the chairs moved back against the walls and the table set with a lace cloth, potato salad, sandwiches, and a bottle of Dubonnet, and while the room was still death cooled and the rest of the living not back yet from the mortuary, so quiet with nobody talking yet, Auntie Girlie and Sis would go up and pour themselves an inch, once they had set out the silverware. Auntie Girlie would let Sis go first and ask, as she lifted her own glass to her lips, "How's your Dubonnet?" Sis would consider before she talked, like she always did, and frown seriously and answer after four or five beats, "How's yours?" in her deep and solemn voice, and they would almost laugh, then laugh. That party after Louis's funeral would be quieter than tonight's, chilly in early afternoon lit by white daylight, light entering in horizontal blocks from the windows, light as penetrating as a bar closing time, and more revealing in its own way. And it would take the aunts Sis and Beryl and Girlie, who would drive together all the way to town from the reservation, and that day even Shirley and Babe, with their ways as tender that afternoon as the flesh on their upper arms, as tough as their eyes as they lifted their chins to point the direction we would walk into that fog of the unseen, that unknown and inevitable future, to warm the room and break that frightening awkward silence, speaking kindly to us, Louis's grandchildren, their words silver strings connecting us to the rest of the family, affirming and confirming our right and proper place among the wounded.

"Here, want to fix a plate for your dad? Take this one with the flowers. Go ask him if he wants a cup of coffee, first."

"You girls all have such pretty hair, so shiny, eh?"

"Look at her. Doesn't she look like Marguerite?" Our grandmother Maggie died before we were born, and we were each of us girls like her, the aunts told us: Artense, who secretly liked pretty things, brave Suzanne, generous Jeannette, graceful Eveline, bashful Jeanne with our dad's quizzical triangular eyes, all of us like our brave, generous, graceful, bashful grandma, who liked pretty things, who'd looked out at the world with those quizzical triangular eyes like our dad's. And she would be, as she had always been for us, missing, *aandakii*, the Ojibwe word for "somewhere else," joined then by our finally eternally missing aandakii somewhere-else grandfather Louis, their absence shockingly tangible, permanently and unexpectedly massive in that bright, cold, cleaned dining room.

1968

But that would be nearly two years into the unseen future that was inevitable as the past: for tonight we were between funerals, and the light in front of the house was yellow, soft through the lampshades in the front room, brighter and sharper in the dining room through the white handkerchief-patterned overhead light fixture. In the kitchen the light was cool blue-white from the florescent ceiling ring, light that thickened and weighted the air, causing the smoke from the cast iron pan of frybread to hover in webs and veils that stuck to our clothes and hair when we walked through the swinging door from the front hallway, where through the beautiful framed oval glass of the front door Uncle Sonny and Uncle George could watch people come up the sidewalk to the front porch, stopping at the door to turn the beautiful egg-shaped iron doorknob, feeling the raised floral design that felt so cool and right, fitting everyone's hand so beautifully. Once in the door, the men slowed or stopped, but the women, their hands full, walked past the old uncles to the swinging kitchen door, into the hazy kitchen, where the aunts and their mother were taking turns at the stove, slowing or stopping only then to talk and drop off what they'd brought—crackers, a bottle of Silver Satin, a saucepan of boiled wieners—and wind up at the dining room table, loaded tonight with food and bottles and cans and ashtrays. When we walked in the house, my mother and I went to the kitchen first, Patsy carrying a plate of her magical peanut cookies, me a bowl of my own specialty, red Jell-O with bananas and whipped cream, passing my father when he stopped by the two old uncles sitting on folding chairs in the hallway, in shadows not touched by the lights. My father said, "Say hello to your uncle Sonny," who raised one bony yellow hand from where it rested on his cane, weighted by a heavy ring with a red stone, "and your Uncle George," who stated solemnly, "I haven't seen you in many moons," and smiled. His smile caused the frame of his glasses, Indian Health Service–issued thick black plastic, to shift crookedly across his wrinkled cheekbones; the heavy glass lenses were two white gibbous moons rising and setting as he nodded slowly.

My boyfriend, Stan, was right behind me. He was a white boy. This was his last night home before he left to go away for college and I'd decided this was it, it was time for him meet the rest of us. "I didn't know Indians really talked like that," he whispered behind me. Uncle George heard. He snapped me a look so quickly that I would have missed it if I hadn't expected it—the two white moons rose again and set and then looked down on the plate of food on his lap—after seeing him take in my boyfriend and his starched oxford cloth button-down-collared shirt with amusement earlier. I was mortified but in love; Stan was an exotic, the son of a minister, and was fascinated by us, our family, our neighborhood, our community; he would learn and eventually become one of us, but how could I know that then, in love but mortified. Stan was going away to college in the morning; he would meet college girls who would be dressed like resurrected Indians, white college girls with pretty teeth, white college girls playing Indian in fringed leather jackets and headbands and beads, while back here in the West End, and up on the rez, at Mozhay Point and at Sweetgrass, we kept on biting the dust.

Cousin Butchie had come in right behind us and stood there with two six-packs of Pabst Blue Ribbon, which he was trying to balance in his left arm so that he could shake hands. Uncle George looked from Stan toward Butch with his lips; Stan understood. He took the beer and led my cousin around several small children, who were playing Candy Land on the floor, and over to the couch. Stan used a church key on the beers for both him and Butch, remembering to be watchful and alert because of what he'd heard about Butchie's being accident prone. So as not to hurt Butch's feelings, Stan clowned, opening the beers with a flourish and presenting Butch's with a deep bow and "Your beer, Sir." Uncle George watched approvingly; I felt relieved.

We didn't want Butch to lose another finger, like he did at the cannery, where he worked, and which wasn't his real job. His real job, his occupation, was to be Butch, waking before the sun each day and stumbling gently through the hours simple and pure in his thoughts and ways, his temperament sweetening what life gave us to chew and swallow. Our job was to watch out for if he held his cigarette backward with the lit end too close to his face and for what was in the chair he was going to sit in and to let him know if he didn't notice the streetlights changing color when he took us out in his car. Stan was doing all right; he didn't point too quickly at anything or call Butchie's attention to things that might cause him to have to turn suddenly and spill his beer or collide with the spirits, motions, and thoughts of other people in the house, tonight or in the past or future.

There was an empty chair at the dining room table, next to a white girl with red hair. She seemed almost asleep, hunched over a plateful of food, her left hand holding her rum and Coke in a circle OK. She raised and turned her head when I pulled out the chair to sit and stared at me with round green eyes that were unmoving, unblinking, and set as marbles in marble for a moment before they began to drift upward and to the left, then back to my face. Shirley, the most sociable of the aunts, said, "Artense, do you know LaDonna Muldoon? She's from next door. Did youse know each other from school?" and stepped into the kitchen, where someone was calling, "Shirley! Where does Babe keep the hot pads?"

The girl stared at me as if horrified but unable to look away, with those unblinking green marble eyes that set, drifted, set, while I took a plate and filled it, stared without speaking when I offered her the bag of potato chips. I realized that she was not frightened, fascinated, or shocked but only physically stunned by the inability of the potato salad and broiled baloney and cheese sandwiches to soak up her rum and Coke at the same speed she'd swallowed it. She finally blinked, as I imagined a turtle would, slowly, enjoying the burn relief of lids over dry eyes, turned to her drink, took a slow-motion sip, turned back to me, and asked, "Hey . . . gotta c-c-c-cigarette?"

"She doesn't smoke," my mother answered for me. She was sitting at the end of the table, perched really, on a kitchen stepstool, with a straight back and an eye I had felt on me as long as I could remember, through walls and over distances and now across Auntie Babe's dining room table.

"What's her name, Muldoon? Muldoon, pleased to meet you." My dad spoke from the window, where he was sitting against the sill, leaning into the window and stretching his legs so that he almost was the same height as if he'd been standing up. He was as amused by LaDonna's name as Uncle George had been by my boyfriend.

"We were in school together, we know each other," I began to explain, and LaDonna turned again, slowly and carefully, to see if she could recognize me, appearing to try to focus each eye separately. Because her head was drooping a little, she turned from one side to the other, using only one eye at a time, toward first my right, then my left breast, then because her hair was beginning to lose its teased and sprayed shape, the bird's nest at the top of her skull sweeping a red wing across her face anyway, that eye disappeared while she thought, "Where would I know her from? Smoking in the girls' bathroom? No. . . . Detention room after that fistfight in the Special Class room? No. . . . Benched in gym class with the rest of us who left our gym suits at home, that's right." Muldoon nodded. "Artense . . . gotta c-c-cigarette?"

THE DAY LOUIS DIED

Two aspirin took twenty minutes to abate the relentless pounding in my jaw, then I could sleep for twenty minutes, until the surge of my heartbeat to the blood vessels below my molar rolled in waves that increased to the inevitable hourly relentless pounding. Walk between the beds to the hall to the bathroom, take two aspirin, wait twenty minutes, sleep twenty, and wake as the tide rose again. Once, as I sat up in bed, knees up, with my hands flat on my knees and my forehead resting on the backs of my hands, Eveline woke and looked at me for a minute, her face turned toward me and her head not moving and her eyes not blinking, just watching me through those eyes brown by day and black by night, and I wondered, would she think this was just a dream, would she remember. She was the third of the sisters, and after high school—that would be six months after Louis's funeral—she would get her first job, working for Mr. Fix-All, who squeezed her rear end every time he passed back of the counter where she clerked, and so she didn't go back after the first day. Then she would go to work at the hospital busing trays and loading the dishwashers and wondering if this was as good as it would get and my mother told her to stay there because maybe she could meet a doctor and get married, which of course was not going to happen, why would a doctor notice some skinny young Indian girl who sure she was pretty but why would he ever look to see her bus his tray after he had left, scrape his plate, and throw out his trash, and besides, she was too bashful to ever look at somebody like that, anyway.

All the last week I had pressed cloves into the hole in my molar every few hours. Relief was burning and sweet smelling, sweet tasting and brief. The last several days I had poured Patsy's recommended treatment, a half-teaspoon of whiskey warmed bowl-side in my hand for a minute, over the tooth, between aspirin doses. When I exhaled that relief expelled in fiery fumes that burned my eyes.

In the dark, watching my sister's eyes slowly close in her worried and pretty face as she fell back asleep, I knew this would have to be the last night.

When I got up in the morning and looked in the mirror, my face was yellow, my eyes two peeholes in the snow, as my mother would say. My jaw was a lemon. My limp and sleep-starved hair shone with oil and clung to my head and neck so that from the back I looked sleek and greasy as an otter. I had thirty dollars, so I called a dentist and took a bus downtown to his office where he handled me too roughly and used both hands to hold the chrome vise he used to twist out my back molar. The dental assistant, a beaten-looking birdlike blonde, reached to hold my hands in hers as he started to pull. He growled at me from his clenched teeth to let go of her hands. She kept her nervously sympathetic blue eyes, forget-me-nots damp and trampled limp on a sidewalk, on mine while he writhed and sweat large teardrop-shaped patches under his arms until with a wrench that pulled my head to the left then the right then the left again he waved my tooth, large, gray-green, long-rooted and bloody, with a hole down the center and side, darkened from the cloves I'd pressed into it, in front of my face. The drained assistant feebly put the tooth into a tiny brown envelope, which I put in my coat pocket, and apologetically charged me eighteen dollars, which left me a girl without a job and twelve dollars to last until I found one. I caught another bus home and rested the left side of my hot face against the cool and greasy window, watching my life thus far, and my father's before me, in the west end of town, rolling dreamscapes of hills, frame houses, corner stores passing across my unmoving and consuming eyes. Artense. Twelve dollars, no job. No Stan, really. Gone to college, dormitory, roommate, nowhere near the West End. Back in the summer, he said. He wasn't really mine, anyway.

When I got home, Patsy had her car coat on, that white corduroy one that she let me borrow once in a while, and the wig I'd bought her when I'd been working, dark blond with light streaks, and a green headband. My dad would be out in front of the house any minute to pick her up. She needed me to watch the kids because they had to go to the hospital. Louis was dead, and somebody was going to have to identify the body. She buried a handful of clean hankies in her coat pocket and fished out a pack of Pep-O-Mint Life Savers. "I know I'm gonna have to be the one to do it; here, have a Life

Saver. Did they pull your tooth? I made hamburger gravy; fix the kids some supper." Her gestures were hesitant, not her usual quick moves that made it look like she was ready for anything, had prepared and practiced and knew what to do; in those gestures I saw and realized that each day was as new for my mother as it was for me, including this one, and that she wasn't really that much older than I was.

She was wearing my sister's tennies and the mood ring my brother bought her at Target (on her it never varied color from the violet blue of serenity and general well-being). Her skin was smooth and tender around her gray eyes. Here's a true story: A neighbor lady said to me once, "You have a beautiful mother, Artense," then did one of those free-association things and said in the next beat that I looked just like my dad. My dad and I still laugh about that, and it's what, how many years ago, now? I always liked to look at my mother and never thought to envy her. And she had some big plans for us all. What they were, neither of us knew. But they were big.

THE PARTY AT AUNT BABE'S

The room was getting noisier, and all that cigarette smoke had softened the yellow light to a gold, swathing and veiling those who hadn't been netted in the kitchen. Somebody who decided to make toast didn't know that the pop-up on the toaster didn't work anymore, and so my eyes began to burn from acrid microparticles of scorched bread. Small bits of red Jell-O that slopped off the spoon as people filled their plates sparkled like rubies on the dining room table until they melted into sticky drops that ran into larger puddles that stuck to the oilcloth. One ashtray, a small tin saucer left by the Stanley salesman, caught fire when Uncle Sonny put out a cigarette against a smoldering empty matchbook on his way through the dining room to look for Uncle George's crossword puzzle book in the kitchen. Uncle Sonny didn't notice, but Cousin Dennis was young and quick and he put it out by pouring a little beer into the ashtray.

A tall man in wool hunting pants and a sleeveless undershirt came through the kitchen door with a bottle of purple wine under his arm and two thick white coffee cups in his hands. He handed one cup, full of black coffee, to Shirley's husband, Ed, who was on the wagon, and nodded to my mother. "Hello, Poddy Jean." They were children together, and he was the only person who could call her that besides her sister, Piggie Onn. My mother, who would nurse her one beer all night, said hello to Rollie and no thanks to a Manischewitz. He stood by her, gaunt and quiet, his skinny arms hanging off his bony shoulders, which hunched a little as he talked with my mother about his wife's long sickness. He drank his wine from a mug, sipping carefully like it was scalding hot coffee, as if he was afraid he'd burn his tongue.

The kitchen door swung open again for a mixed-blood James Dean, handsome in his ducktail haircut, muscular, short, with a barrel chest, slender legs, and beefy arms, which stretched the rolled-up sleeves of his white T-shirt. He said hello to Shirley and asked about her mother's broken hip, how was it healing, was she getting around, holding Shirley's hand while he talked, and then for a few seconds more, like she was sixteen years old. His dark hair, navy blue eyes, brown arms, and white teeth were dazzling. His engineer boots made a deep and hollow stamping sound as he walked over to our end of the table. At a powwow last summer, I had watched those boots do a two-step version of that same walk, those shoulders of his dipping slightly first to the left, then to the right, suspended on a separate plane above his forward-facing hips and bowed legs as he danced. Across the powwow circle a fancy shawl dancer in blue and silver had accelerated her hop, raising her knees and lengthening her steps, nearly sprinting to catch up behind him so she could watch.

"Frankie. . . . Frankie, how you been?" LaDonna jerked her head up and became almost animated, her smile big and fuzzy as her voice. "Frankie, what you drinking there?" Frankie stood behind us and leaned over so that his head was between mine and LaDonna's, resting his upper body weight on his hands, one on the back of each of our chairs. I imagined his chest muscles jumped, inches from the back of my head. "Frankie, you want a rum and Coke?" She folded her hands on the table and leaned forward over them, as though praying, then straightened and swayed into the back of her chair, looking up in further supplication.

Aunt Babe carried in another cookie sheet of hot sandwiches, split hamburger buns with broiled cheese and sliced olives arranged on top, which she placed on the dining room table. Frankie inhaled deeply. "Doesn't that smell great?"

LaDonna shuddered and lowered her head to the table.

"Babe, you fussed. Look at that, Patsy. Daughter, you really fussed," admired Babe's mother and our family's matriarch from the easy chair that Rollie pulled up to the table for her. Grandma Lisette had stopped frying sliced baloney ring and frybread in the kitchen, turned off the stove, and was ready to enjoy herself. Her plate was full, her shiny face round as the plate and damp from work, unlined and happy. "Patsy, try yourself one of those pretty sandwiches. Look, they're just toasty and crispy looking."

My mother picked one up between her thumb and first finger and took a small bite, then her third sip of beer of the evening. "Babe, these are the best tuna sandwiches I ever ate."

"That's because it's chicken."

Rollie got up from his place next to me, excusing himself, "Forgot to say hello to Sonny," and Frankie sat in the chair he vacated. "Hi, Artense."

Artense. My name. He could have said it under so many different circumstances. He pulled me out of the way just as I stepped off the sidewalk in front of a car, and said it again and again out of relief and gratitude for my life—Artense. He kissed me and was nearly out of breath with the experience—Artense. He asked to spend the rest of his life by my side, where he could watch me adore his dancing—Artense.

"Hi, Frankie," I smiled, my head down, and thought about what else I could say that could continue this conversation. I was nearly eighteen, almost a woman, and should finally be able to talk with him as a woman would to a man. I raised my head and inhaled, waiting for words to continue.

"What do you do now, you done with school? You working?" The moment had passed me by but Frankie was considerate enough to continue and take me with him.

"She's going to start going to the junior college this fall," my mother answered for me.

"Oh." Frankie, his turn to be the tongue-tied one, thought for a moment. I could see him searching for something to say to somebody so impressive and foreign. "Do you like Manischewitz?"

"She doesn't drink," replied Patsy.

THE DAY LOUIS DIED

The police had found Louis lying where he had fallen, in a half-frozen puddle in the alley behind the Stevedore Surf and Turf, where Stan and I had gone to eat after the prom. While Louis was still conscious, he was able to tell them my dad's name. Then his lungs congested and filled quickly with pneumonia, what they used to call the Old People's Friend, and he died not long after they brought him to the hospital. Just like she'd thought, my mother had to be the one to identify the body, to tell the police that it was Louis, and she had to be the one to take his wallet from his pants pocket. Inside, there was nothing but my graduation picture. No money, no social security card. Just a black-and-white wallet-sized picture of me. A high school graduation picture, the first graduate in our entire family, and so a very big deal. I suppose that when he put it in the plastic sleeve we must have looked at one another face to face. Louis, unbroken by twentieth-century America and federal Indian policies, the Indian boarding school, alcohol, jobs hard and dangerous and impermanent, a life's playing field set on the edge of a cliff. Louis, on that day as he would be on the day of his funeral, handsome still in a used coat and green pants from the county work farm. Louis the soft-voiced incorrigible. And his granddaughter Artense in black and white, perching on the photographer's wooden stool the same way my mother sat, ready to fly, in a secondhand sweater, hair shingled and teased on top, smile a mask that almost did the job. Artense, who did as she was told and would graduate from high school. Artense, unbroken but yet untested. He was fifty when I was born. A half-century gap in our experiences. Fifty years. Our lives coincided for less than twenty.

THE CLASS OF 1968

Frankie found something he could say to a girl who would be going to college. "So, Artense, what class did you like the best in school?" He had poured four fingers of purple Manischewitz into a glass decorated with decals of flying ducks and opened a can of Coke for me with the little church key attached to his nail clippers. "Did you take history? I used to like history. Did you study about George Washington? What did you think of him? Do you know that some people think he was a better president than Abraham Lincoln? Why would they think that? What do you think about that, Artense?" I was tongue-tied. Frankie was flirting with me—with me! And he must have been five or ten years older than I was, I thought. A man. He'd been in the navy, and he'd been around the country, and he worked at the packing plant, and he'd bought his mother a color TV, and he rode a motorcycle. A man. I could see over the neckline of his white undershirt that his chest was smooth, with a few delicately curling damp-looking tendrils of hair, and when he reached across me to pour a little Coke into LaDonna's empty glass ('Frankie! Frankie, how are you doing? Where's the rum?" she pulled one hand out from under her head to pat his arm, tender-looking skin the color of vanilla caramel), I could see below the stretching sleeves of his clean T-shirt delicately curling damp-looking tendrils of hair in his armpits as well. He smelled like cigarettes, wine, and spearmint gum. I looked down at my lap, then, because he was turned toward LaDonna, over at his. His jeans looked new, crisp dark blue and rolled up on the bottom. I turned around and could see on the front room couch Stan steadying Butchie's hand, the one holding the can of beer, which Butchie was waving as he made a point. Stan had no chest hair. He was still a boy. His pants were chinos, with creases. His sister ironed his shirts, his mother sorted his socks. He would be leaving in the morning to go away to a real college and live in a dormitory. At almost eighteen, how could I know that one day he would be one of us? All I knew at the time was that he was going to leave. At almost eighteen, what I did know was that he wasn't really mine, any more than Frankie was.

Frankie unrolled a pack of Marlboros from his T-shirt sleeve and flicked it toward me with a little snap of his wrist (bone and muscle flexed, knit), and two cigarettes (one for me and one for him!) neatly slid out, just like in the commercials. "Artense, sugaswaa?"

I looked over to my mother's perch, which was empty. I reached for the cigarette.

"Frankie? Frankie, you want . . . hey, Frankie." Frankie turned toward LaDonna, who was looking at the ceiling now trying to remember what she started to say, concentrating, thinking so hard that she looked sober. From her point of balance, the balls of her feet planted on the floor, she tipped her head farther and farther back as she looked up and up at the light fixture then beyond that and suddenly LaDonna, though still in her chair, was on the floor, lying on her back, her plaid skirt flipped up so that her underpants showed, big white ones so loose they looked all creased and dented, above her long skinny white legs, and she realized where she was and looked at Frankie and me, so surprised, and I reached down to pull her skirt to cover those underpants (they're so big, I thought; they must be her mother's). She didn't say a word. Frankie quickly tipped her chair back upright. She smiled then, seeing the room back where it was had been, and laughed just once, a fuzzy blue chuckle.

"Muldoon." From the windowsill, my dad called her name. "Frankie. Did Muldoon get knocked out?"

"She's good, Buster, just lost her balance is all, didn't you. You're good, aren't you, LaDonna?" said Frankie. LaDonna leaned back into his arm that was across the back of her chair. She was smitten.

"Muldoon," said my dad, "you're going to be all right."

THE FOURTH DAY

Aunt Babe's house was quiet and cold after the funeral, and the air clear, no smoke from frybread or cigarettes, a sharpness of clarity painful to inhale and painful to look through. Louis's sister, Lisette, sat on a chair out in the kitchen; she had waved her daughters and nieces away as she would a flock of seagulls. No, she liked it in the kitchen. She would come out in a little while. Dennis, home from basic training, half knelt at her side, on one knee, holding her hand that rested on his other knee. In his army uniform he looked like Louis when he played the trumpet in the band at Harrod boarding school, Lisette thought to herself. Remember that picture she used to have of Louis in his boarding school uniform, holding his trumpet? Whatever happened to that picture? It was a picture postcard, remember, that he had addressed to his mother but never sent. He had left it for her under the door to the girls' dormitory, the last time he ran away from school. Above the high collar of his uniform coat with the braid and the buttons his face was stern and serious, so unlike him. He held the trumpet upright on his knee, like a bayonet; she had thought that Louis looked like a soldier. "Like Dennis," she thought, as she sat holding her grandson's adult hand. They had the same mouth, smooth and full, tender, red lipped, and snub nose, and those dark gray-brown eyes that almost looked blue. The same round moon face, with the same deep cowlick like a whirlwind above the left eye. Dennis and young Louis.

"Want some coffee, Grandma? I'll get you some." Dennis looked into her face, and she thought how he used to do that when he was small, standing where he now knelt, at the same chair, his feet on the outside of hers, his forearms on her knees, his face so like Louis's as he looked right into hers, that mannerism Dennis's alone, so unlike Louis yet so essentially Louis. She nodded yes and reached to wipe a cake crumb off her grandson's lower lip. He rose gracefully, tall and adult in his army uniform, poured a cup of coffee from the pot on the stove, added canned milk and sugar, and knelt again next to her chair. He held her soft old hand in his again, and she remembered little Dennis's small, star-shaped hand holding hers while they walked to the store, to the post office, to school on the first day, a little boy's hand that fit inside hers.

Louis's hand had been that same size when he started school. The huddle of children had been herded off the train at the Harrod train depot by the school's disciplinarian, a man who carried a doubled leather strap that he absently, menacingly waved back and forth. He lined them up in pairs, shortest first, tallest last, to get on the wagon that would take them to the boarding school. The smallest boy, Louis, was led by his big sister, Lisette, to the front of the line, where she gently removed his hand, trusting and damp, from her own and joined it with the hand of the smallest girl. As she walked to her own place at the end of the line, the little boy turned his head to watch, stepping from the line, still holding the hand of the little girl.

"Stay with your partners," the disciplinarian said sternly. He tapped the little boy's shoulder with the strap, then slapped it with a wet sound against the palm of his hand.

Miles away, and further away by the minute, a teenage boy drove a hearse up the county road to the cemetery. In the back, inside the coffin, Louis wore my dad's clothes, his suit and shirt and tie and socks (he didn't really need shoes, the mortician said; that wouldn't show). The mortician's son sang with his favorite radio station on the ride and said to the coffin in back, "You don't mind if I turn this up, do you?"

Louis watched us from the great distance that he had covered over the past four days of his long and arduous walk westward to the next life.

At the end of the fourth day, she was waiting on the other side of the last river, among the stars, her dark hair neatly knotted at the back of her neck, her white blouse reflecting the silver-blue of starlight. The night wind blew and lifted her dark skirt to one side; below, her small feet, which were laced severely at the ankles in ladies' boots, like a teacher's, stepped closer to the shore; the heels left the ground as she rose to her toes, clasping her hands as if in prayer. The sight filled his eyes as he waded into the river and swam; then as his feet touched bottom again he nearly galloped through the cold and heavy current. The rocks on the shore warmed and dried his feet those last steps.

"Maggie," he said, his feet light as smoke. "Maggie."

"Nishimoshe, my sweetheart," Maggie sang in her light and silvery voice, "a long time I have waited for you to come over to where I am."

"Wijiiwagan," he answered, and folded his hands over hers, covering her prayers with his own.

And so Louis joined his true love, Maggie, and they joined the others who watch us from far beyond where the sun sets, the past that birthed the present that even now births the future. They pray as we pass into life, they pray us through our lives, they pray as we pass out of life; when we die, they pray our steps across the walk west. Thus blessed, we live and die in an air hung with their prayers, the breath of their words on our faces and bodies, their spirits among us, trying to see and hear and understand. Wegonen, what is it, we think. Amanj i dash, and I wonder. We ponder this all of our lives, not realizing what we already know.

SHONNUD'S GIRL

1936

The horses lived on the other side of the wooden fence at the edge of Mr. McCuskey's farm, in their own horse paradise of woods and meadow and barn. Violet and I secretly rode them from time to time both summers we lived there, in the meadow that like the McCuskey farm was lost in forfeit to the county for back taxes not long after Mrs. McCuskey took Violet and after little Sam and I went to the orphanage. For decades now the horse paradise has been the jail and work farm, and McCuskey's farm the nursing home, where Lisette lives.

Lisette was my mother's dearest friend; she used to call me Rosie-ens or Sister-ens or "my little niece," but now she thinks I am a ghost. When I call her Auntie, her mind searches through all the relatives and friends who still live in her head; not finding me frightens her.

Going into Duluth when we drive down from the reservation to visit Lisette at the old folks' home, we pass the prisoners who work outside on the farm or on the grounds of the home. Some of the men who get caught breaking the law and have to do their time get to work with the horses there, maybe even ride them, when nobody's looking, like me and Violet. But we were never caught.

Once in a while, on afternoons that we thought that our mother would be all right without us for a while, that she was going to stay home, that she was not going to leave us, we would sneak away from the house to meet the horses there at the fence, Violet and I. We waited on Mr. McCuskey's side of the fence. The first summer, Violet was tall enough to stand with her forearms and folded hands on the top rail, her chin on her hands; the second summer, I could do the same, stretching so that my dress, one of those skimpy cotton wash dresses that little girls wore during those days of the Great Depression, pulled up, and my bloomers showed. From the fence we could see all the way to the edge of paradise, where the horses stood under the tamaracks. We never called them; they seemed to sense us: their bodies would become very still, their necks would stiffen; ripples ran across their sides like those tiny waves on their drinking pond during steady wind. I wonder now if they watched for us, too, but obliquely, like Ojibwe people do. The obliqueness of a horse's gaze is a necessity, because of the way its eyes have been placed by God, for reasons we will only understand after we die, if we still care to know. The obliqueness of an Ojibwe's gaze is also a necessity, because of what transpired after we were moved from where God had placed us. The gaze of an aandakii Ojibwe, who lives elsewhere, beyond even that, is the most oblique of them all.

We never called them. They approached us, the beautiful horses, when the time—given to us and meant to be by the Great Spirit who is God—was right, slowly and indirectly, gliding toward us in figure eights around the trees, appearing, disappearing, reappearing, until they came up to the fence and stuck their noses through to be petted. We would stand up on our toes to reach their foreheads, stroking them from between their eyes down to their nostrils, while they stood perfectly still, those beautiful horses, each more breath-taking than the last. We were in love with them all and never could have chosen one over the other—the brown with white spots, the almost black with the white blaze forehead, the round, short-legged pony, the light brown with the maroon eyes like our mother's, the old faded gray, blind in one eye. They chose favorites, however: the almost black liked me the best; the light brown liked Violet.

From behind the fence we could, by moving from side to side, look between the trees all the way to the owners' house and barn and the pickup truck parked in the yard. Sometimes if the truck was gone we would walk along the fence almost to the house and coax a couple of those horses all along the fence to where their woods ended and the meadow began and then creep under the fence. We walked toward them slowly, speaking softly in baby talk, one hand out. They stood still, their eyes focused somewhere above our heads while they listened, knowing what we wanted and what we would do next. Close enough to touch, we patted their noses, so lightly; they tolerated our little girl hands as we stepped slowly and gently to their sides, talking and stroking noses, necks, then sides. Our little girl voices rang high and husky in the stillness of the owners' absence, the horses' breaths a lower pitch in the stillness of their waiting.

I always went first; that's how it was with me and Violet. When the patting and soothing, the soft urging of our young voices, and the warm low-pitched breathing of the horses blended into an almost audible hum of anticipation, I grasped the almost black's mane in both hands and swung my right leg up across his back, belly-flopping the front of my body, elbows bent, face buried in the base of his neck where his mane ended; then, with my arms, I pushed myself upright, sitting astride, the skirt of my dress tucked tightly under my legs from the front, floating in a washed cotton puff out the back. Because Violet's legs were longer, she always went up a little more easily, a little more gracefully; her slender, straight back and her long neck looked like a natural extension of the horse. As I have thought of her over the years, I have imagined Violet like that all through her life, wherever she has lived it, even today if she is still alive, sitting gracefully and lightly atop whatever life gives her to ride on, chin high, eyes quizzical, mouth smiling shyly. To me, she was beautiful in the way our mother was. I don't know if anyone else saw her that way.

Our mother. We never knew and never thought to wonder what it was that would cause her to leave those afternoons, because whatever it was, it was beyond our understanding and hers. There in the middle of listening to the radio, or rocking the baby, or stirring something on the stove, the tremor of her being would slow for just a few seconds and she would be still, as if hearing something of a softness or pitch beyond her children's ears, put down the baby, or the spoon, or the mop, and walk out the door and down the road. If it was cold she stepped into the bedroom first, reaching into the closet for her coat, the brown cloth one that she buttoned the little fur collar to in the winter. Summers, she just took off her apron and hung it on the nail by the stove and left, walked out the door and down the road all along the McCuskeys' farm and the horse paradise and didn't look back.

Up until that one time, she always came back, though. She had no place else she could stay.

Our mother. The white people, except for our dad, called her by her boarding school name, Charlotte. Everybody else called her Shonnud. Thin—she was always thin—and big boned. And nervous, people said, with that tremor beating and quivering under her skin, her fingers always moving so slightly I still wonder to this day if I saw it, or heard, or felt. I suppose she was homely, with that bony, long-jawed face and those eyes of hers, long, triangular, maroon, and looking off to the side, the side her head tilted down toward, the side that her trembling wide and thin-lipped mouth turned down toward, the side she turned away from the world. Her left side. Her left shoulder dipped slightly; her right shoulder rose. Perennially oblique, her stance stepped its quarter turn away though she faced forward, her elbows out, the backs of her hands facing front. As she walked down the road away from us she looked forlorn, blown off course, on days windy or still, her walk seemingly aimless, her destination somewhere down that road.

We never asked her to stay. We never asked her where she was going, knowing as we did that it was beyond our understanding and hers. When we were little and still living downtown, Cousin Cynthia sometimes took care of us while our mother was gone; when Cynthia went away to school, Violet and I became girls big enough to take care of ourselves and Daddy when she left. And Sam, after he was born.

As I can recall, it always happened in the afternoon. There were the afternoons before she left. The afternoons she walked out the door. The afternoons she was gone. The afternoons she came back weren't afternoons at all; they were the dark-clouded dawns, really, of long days of waiting for her next departure.

We never asked her where she had been, when she came walking back up the road a few days later, tired and pale. If it was cold, she stepped into the bedroom first, reaching into the closet to hang up her coat and smooth it out with shaky hands before lying down to rest. She lay on her back, in the middle of the bed she shared with our father, hands folded on her stomach, fingers trembling, eyes sometimes open, sometimes closed, narrow nose and feet pointed at the ceiling. Her body sank into the dip in the middle of the bed and appeared to flatten just about down to the height of the mattress.

She breathed so quietly that we held our own breaths in order to hear her.

Our dad found out she'd left when he came in from working the farm, to a scrubbed kitchen in a quiet house. He never asked, "Where's your mother?" Maybe that first time he did, asked Cynthia, but he never asked Violet and me, just went to the sink to wash and sat at the table for his supper. We dished it up for him, just as Mother did when she was home, and he ate it silently. If he wanted more, we could tell, and we dished it on his plate. He ate without talking, everything on his plate, then wiped up whatever was left with a piece of bread, chewed and swallowed, wiped his mouth with the back of his hand.

When Mother was gone, Violet and I became the mothers to the baby, Sam. He slept with us in our parents' bed, and our dad slept on the kitchen floor, rolled in a blanket, next to the stove, where Violet and I slept when Mother was home. Our dad got up early to help Mr. McCuskey and didn't want anybody to fix his breakfast or talk to him; he didn't even want to see anybody when Mother was gone. We stayed in bed and kept Sam quiet until after our dad had left to work.

We lived in the two-room house built by the Bjornborgs, who homesteaded the property long before the McCuskeys bought it. Mr. Bjornborg, his young wife, and her nephew had put up a shed first, where they lived with the animals for the first couple of years, and when they built the house it was on the little trail that led to the shed, which they added on to and made into a barn. When we lived there our father worked for Mr. McCuskey, who lived in the new house he had built for Mrs. McCuskey and all the children they had hoped for, and the trail was a county road. The Bjornborgs' first barn had burned down years before the McCuskeys ever moved there. The Bjornborgs' second son died trying to rescue the cow. We never walked on that spot.

Today, of course, nobody even remembers the McCuskeys but me. The prisoners work in a big concrete-floored barn where the Bjornborgs' house was.

When our dad got hired to work for Mr. McCuskey it was a good chance for us to live in the country. He was handy and good with animals and thought he was lucky to leave the scrap yard for the chance to work the farm, with free rent included. The house had a bedroom and a kitchen and a lean-to shed off the back of the kitchen. The outhouse, next to the Bjornborgs' old one that had been filled up and shoveled over and made into a toolshed, was almost new, dug by Mr. McCuskey. When we moved into the old and empty house, I could just about see a ghost path from the house to the old outhouse that had become the toolshed, an ever so slight bareness in the quack grass where the ghosts of the ill-fated Bjornborgs must brush, cutting their vapor feet as they moved back and forth, back and forth in the night, looking for the outhouse. I shivered and carried the bag of my and Violet's clothes into the house that, inside, didn't look haunted at all. Mrs. McCuskey had washed the windows and swept and dusted and put new paper on the long shelf above the stove, which she folded into fancy squares and points along the edge. She had scrubbed the floors and walls and cleaned and blacked the woodstove. On the kitchen table, which she had painted apple green, was a plateful of doughnuts, so many that they were not quite covered by a white dishtowel that she had tucked over them. We moved into the old Bjornborg house after Sam was born. We fit fine in the house, Violet and I sleeping on the kitchen floor, Sam in the bedroom with our mother and dad.

Dad slept holding our mother's trembling hands in both of his. On the good days, she woke early, before everyone; on those days the smell of the coffee woke us up, and we opened our eyes to watch from where we'd slept on the floor her skinny ankles and feet do little dancing turns around the floor while she stirred oatmeal, took the lugallette out of the oven, set out bowls and spoons. "Kwesensag, ambe wiisinin," she all but sang in her quiet and thin voice, smiling and as scrubbed and neatly combed as Mrs. McCuskey. "Ondii Baby-ens? Wiisinii-daa!"

Every day but Sunday, Daddy worked for Mr. McCuskey until suppertime. He plowed, planted, harvested, took care of the horses and cows, repaired the barn and the house, kept the yards clean, and sometimes hired out with Mr. McCuskey on other farms or to do roadwork. Violet and I helped our mother with Sam and the house and helped Mrs. McCuskey with the chickens. We had what seemed like the entire outdoors to play in. And on the other side of the fence was the horse paradise. It was a big improvement over our apartment in Duluth.

DULUTH

When we lived in Duluth, Cynthia didn't live with us. She was away at school with her friend Ernestine at the Tomah Indian college in Wisconsin, where they were becoming educated ladies. Ernestine had already graduated and had a paying job in the kitchen and her own room, and Cynthia was working at her outing placement, taking care of the laundry and small children for a family in Prairie du Chien. That summer right after school ended they took the train to visit us in Duluth, when we lived in that apartment in the West End, on the same block as the Robineau brothers, and stayed with us for two weeks.

Ernestine didn't have a family.

Ernestine had a peach-colored dress, still new looking, that she had made for graduation, with money that she had earned herself from her own outing placement.

Dear Superintendent Ripp:

I am requesting $12.00 from my work placement savings account to buy fabric, thread, and trim for summer dresses and under-clothing for Cynthia Sweet and me. My dress will be worn for the graduation ceremony and will wear nicely for summer also. Cynthia is in need of a new summer dress as she has outgrown the one she has been wearing. I have nearly $40.00 in my ac-count from my earnings, which after the $12.00 will be more than enough for train tickets for our visit to Cynthia's home this summer.

Sincerely,

Ernestine Gunnarson

Dear Miss Gunnarson

You may spend $7.00 on materials for your summer dress and underclothing. See the attendant in the discipline office for the money, which I have placed in an envelope for that use. Miss Sweet will receive a new summer-weight work uniform, which will suffice for her needs; however, because the $7.00 should be more than enough for your clothing expenses, you may buy ad-ditional trim for the summer dress you wore last year. You and Cynthia may turn and trim the dress, which will become hers for church and town.

Alma Ripp, Superintendent of Girls

Ernestine and Cynthia cleaned the apartment for Mother and washed and ironed and patched our clothes. They were kind to us and worked to bring a little of the order from Tomah to our lives, but they didn't have a lot to say to us; mostly, they spoke to each other. They didn't say more than two words to our dad. They stepped back or to the side when they passed him in the hallway, looking away to the side. Cynthia's dad had left her with us just like that, gone to Minneapolis, when she was younger than Violet and I were. So our dad was the only one she had.

When she was old enough for school, a social worker came to the apartment one day and left with Cynthia; the next day Violet and I walked to the depot with Mother to wave to Cynthia as she left on the train. We didn't know why, Violet and I, and couldn't ask Mother, who was walking in her sleep that day, her cheeks puffy and her eyes and nose swollen and pink from the wine she had been drinking the night before.

We didn't find out about our dad's prison record until Sam enlisted in the army. I suppose the county couldn't let a little girl live with a person like that unless she was his own child. But he was always good to Cynthia, and to Violet, Sam, and me. And almost always to our mother.

Cynthia visited us in the summers and wrote a letter to Mother once a month. She and Ernestine lived in a dormitory, where every girl had her own bed and her own trunk to keep her letters and things in, and they had these sharp-looking Sunday uniforms with braid on the collar and chevrons on the sleeves and striped ticking work dresses they made themselves in sewing class to wear while they earned their keep. They went to football games and lyceums. They saw a ballet once. There was a matron in charge of the girls; she was supposed to take care of them. She made sure they had clean clothes and neat hair and made their beds and kept the place nice and acted like ladies. It was her job. She lived in a room in the dormitory and slept there every night so they were never left alone. That was her job.

At the end of their last summer at home, Mother left late in the afternoon, on the day before Ernestine and Cynthia went back to Tomah. We were hanging out the open front room window to look at the jail, watching a policeman walk a swaying and resigned drunk toward the sandstone steps to sleep it off in a cell. At the bottom of the steps, the drunk stopped and looked down at his feet, then turned from the waist and looked up at the sky and freedom and the little girls hanging out the window and waved. The policeman put one arm around the drunk's waist and held his other hand; the two of them turned and walked up the steps as if they were dancing or ice skating. As they walked through the door into the jail, our mother walked through the door out of our apartment.

Violet and I stood by the door staring at Ernestine and Cynthia, who would know what to do next. They stared back, and thought, and looked at each other. Then Ernestine said, "Well, let's finish cleaning this place up."

"It's a dump," answered Cynthia. "Look at it. We can't even wash the walls, the plaster's all crumbling." She ran her hand along one bare patch, and white grains sprinkled like powdery sand to the floor. "All you could do with this is cover it up." Again she and Ernestine looked at each other, young women becoming educated ladies. Then they walked into the bedroom, this their last afternoon of their last visit home. Cynthia pulled Mother's money bag from the hole in the mattress, where she kept it hidden, and counted out nearly three dollars. "Ernestine, my girl," she said, "go see if the Robineau boys are home. We're gonna wallpaper this place."

The Robineau boys brought over a bottle of their homemade brew and a lard bucket filled with flour to make paste. Cynthia and Ernestine used part of the flour to mix a pan of lugallette. When it was baked, Violet and I sat on the bed in the front room and watched them work and party; I remember it like it was yesterday. They drank the brew right from the bottle, and we ate the lugallette slice by slice, spreading each one with a little lard and sprinkling it with the sugar that Cynthia bought with the money left over from the wallpaper. They mixed the rest of the flour with water in the bucket and spread it on the back of each wallpaper section that Johnny measured and cut. They shared that one bottle of brew the whole time they did this, and as the night went on they got silly and started laughing hard at anything anybody said, and George said, "Look at the wallpaper, it's all crooked," which made them all laugh harder. Ernestine and Johnny began to dance, their hands and the front of Ernestine's apron all crusted with drying flour paste, and Cynthia and George sat on the bed next to Violet and me, singing and clapping to keep time.

"Come on, Sissy, let's dance," Ernestine said to me, and took my hands. We swung and twirled, then Johnny grabbed Violet around the waist and carried her around the room, dancing with only his feet on the floor, her feet dangling near his knees. We were delighted with the attention; I watched the room tilt and spin as Ernestine held me by one hand and twirled me one direction, then the other. Violet smiled as Johnny hefted her weight a little higher, dancing with her behind sitting on his right forearm, his left hand holding her hand out like they were in a ballroom, and when Ernestine and Johnny got too tired to dance us around anymore we all fell right onto the bed, and George and Cynthia got up to dance.

George held Cynthia tightly, pulling her left hand behind his back, laying his cheek against hers, and she put her hands against his chest and pushed. "Cut that out, you!" she scolded, which offended him, so he went back to wallpapering, leaning against the wall while he did it so he could hold the bottle in one hand and wallpaper with the other.

Violet and I fell asleep while they were still partying, and when we woke up it was morning, the overhead light was still on, and the Robineau boys were asleep on the floor. Cynthia was packing the suitcases and Ernestine was wetting down the wallpaper so it would come off the wall. She cleaned the flour mess up and shook Johnny by the shoulder. "Johnny, you and George gotta fix this wallpaper."

Daddy came back that afternoon; during the times Cynthia was visiting he never slept at the apartment when Mother was gone. By the time he arrived, the place was clean, Ernestine and Cynthia had left for the train station, and Johnny and George were getting the wallpaper on good and straight.

I wouldn't see Cynthia again for a long time.

AT THE WORK FARM

When Daddy got the job with Mr. McCuskey, he left the scrap yards for good and we moved out of the West End, all of us, Daddy, Mother, Violet, baby Sam, and me, out to the country. Violet and I loved living at the farm, loved Mrs. McCuskey, who waved at us when she was out hanging her wash. Her windburned, reddened face shone as bright and happy as the sun below her frilled mop cap; her spotless white sheets hung in bleached brilliance below the bright and happy McCuskey farm's sun. She had us over for coffee and caramel rolls, treated our mother like special company, me and Violet like ladies, snuggled Sam in her lap and smelled his head, and told us how they were hoping to have a little one of their own one of these days, she and the Mister. And she and the Mister treated us kindly, always kindly. A couple of times when Mother actually woke them up in the middle of the night screaming unspeakable things as she and Dad shoved and hit each other, Mrs. McCuskey wrapped our blankets around the three of us children and brought us to her own house, putting me and Violet to bed in her guest bedroom, between sheets (they were so smooth, so clean, so fragrant), our heads on pillowcases she had embroidered with pansies, and slept with Sam in her own bed while Mr. McCuskey, a massive man, made pots of coffee while he calmed our parents in the same pretty McCuskey kitchen where we had been special company.

"I didn't touch her, sir," Dad told him in a shaky voice. "Shonnud, you crazy Indian, tell him I didn't touch you."

Mother stood gripping the back of a kitchen chair, too overwrought to sit or speak, in her coat that Mrs. McCuskey had wrapped around her shoulders for modesty ("Here, Charlotte, here, put this on, I'll take your kiddies to my house tonight. Here, Charlotte, put on your coat"), in her nightgown so thin and worn it was nearly transparent, her eyes downcast, her face shiny with sweat, her hair black snakes writhing round her long damp neck.

"Mrs. Sweet, come on now, you can either sit down and have some coffee, or you can go home and go to bed," Mr. McCuskey growled in his deep voice.

She stood silently, frightfully, knuckles sharp white bones showing through the skin of her hands. He repeated himself. She raised her eyes and nearly unnerved him with her unfocused purple glare.

"My God, poor Sweet," he thought. "I mean it, Mrs. Sweet, one or the other, take your pick."

She went to bed.

"I swear, sir, I didn't touch her," Dad lied again.

"Maynard, man, let's have some of that coffee."

Violet and I lay awake in the guest bed for a long time. To this day I wish I could enjoy fresh, ironed sheets and pillowcases the way other people do. But I don't. It causes me to feel dread and suffer insomnia. Long nights I have, sometimes, remembering that beautiful bed. We lay awake, Violet and I, until she fell asleep, and for once she went first, slept with the side of her face against that white pillowcase, her mouth in sleep turned down on that side. She lay on her left side, facing me, right shoulder down, left up and forward. She looked beautiful in the way our mother was. I watched her sleep.

But those were the bad nights. Things weren't always bad. There were the days Mother was up before Dad and cooked and cleaned and swept and hung the blankets out on the clothesline to air out. There were the days she put on her good dress, the white one with the low waist and embroidery down by the hem on the left side, and brought us over to Mrs. McCuskey's for coffee (our Mother had lovely manners that she had learned at boarding school, the one run by the mission, and the sight of Mother's slender, long-boned hands stirring sugar into one of Mrs. McCuskey's delicate wedding china cups contrasted so with Mrs. McCuskey's red, work-roughened hands that were heavy as a man's). And there was that one day she had me take her to the dump.

Her eyes were bright that late summer morning; the floor was mopped and the windows were open to air the rooms. Violet and I were out in the yard with Sam, and she called to me, "Sister, go get the wagon! We're going to the dump!"

In those days it wasn't an unusual thing for people to go out to the dump to see what they could find, and it wasn't unusual for a girl like me, and I was only ten, to drive a wagon. So I hitched up Sugar Pie, the mule, to Mr. McCuskey's wagon that he kept in our yard, harnessed up like I'd seen Dad do, and Mother and I went up the road way out in the country to the dump. Like I said, it wasn't an unusual thing, and in those days people went to the dump to get all kinds of things.

It was a nice day; the breeze that was airing out our house was airing out the whole outside, and Mother and I could smell the barn, and then the creek, and then we thought there must some sweetgrass close by. Sugar Pie's rear shone in the sun; the mule tossed her head as she trotted up the county road. I held the reins and didn't really need to do anything; Sugar Pie acted like she knew the road and was going someplace she really liked (we always called Sugar Pie "she" because Mrs. McCuskey said she was a girl no matter what anybody else said). She actually pranced as we got to the dump turnoff and stopped willingly when Mother found a good place for us to stop. And it was a good day at the dump. There were a lot of people there, people who knew us.

"Shonnud, my girl, are you looking for a dresser?" called Old Man Shigog. "There's a pretty nice one here."

"Boozhoo, Uncle. No, thank you," my mother called back politely, "but if I hear of anybody who is, I'll tell them about it."

My mother hopped around the dump in her black strap pumps like she was sixteen years old, her skinny legs in her black stockings almost skipping from one spot to the next. The day was so warm that she rolled her stockings down to just below her knees, which I could see flash white in the sun as she climbed hills of refuse. Her hair began to loose from its bun and hang in strings on each side of her face, which began to take on some color from her exertions. She smiled her crooked smile and laughed, a songbird it sounded like, with the other people at the dump. She introduced me proudly, "Mrs. Bigboy, this is my girl, Rose. Rose, Mrs. Bigboy knew you when you were a baby. . . . Yes, she is getting to be a young woman now, isn't she. . . . Yes, very pretty. . . . Yes, we are very proud of her."

"Young woman, you take good care of your mother," Mrs. Bigboy directed me as we went on to another refuse pile.

We found a straight chair that was in very nice shape, and Mother told me that was all we should take since we didn't really need anything else. At a clean grassy spot we ate the bread we'd brought in a basket, along with some crabapples we picked on the way to the dump. Mother lay on her back, hands folded at her waist, looking from me to the clouds. "When your dad gets his money from Mr. McCuskey this Friday I think I might be able to buy some material for new dresses for you and Violet," she said, although she and I both knew this wasn't possible. "What color do you like?" We talked about what colors would look the best on each, dark red on me, a blue plaid on Violet, and how a green print would look on the dress my mother might make for herself sometime, too, until the sun became so bright overhead that she closed her eyes. I watched her as she slept. She looked like Violet.

We decided to take a shortcut on the way home and followed this road that was paved almost to the outskirts of town. Here I was, ten years old and coming back from the dump with a sleepy mother with grass in her hair and a straight chair in very nice shape, driving a mule with Mr. McCuskey's farm wagon on a street right in the middle of town, almost in the middle of all those cars. "Hey! Hey, youse! Go back to the reservation!" a young man in a flivver shouted. I drew my elbows tightly to my sides and put my head down, looking only at Sugar Pie's shiny backside and what I could see between her big ears of the street. Mother sat with oblique dignity, left shoulder dipping slightly, right shoulder up, her long neck gracefully holding her head with chin high, eyes quizzical, mouth smiling shyly, crookedly, looking around at the houses and buildings without a sign that she could see anyone looking at the sight of her and her little girl and Sugar Pie, her demeanor and manners as lovely as if she were sitting sipping sweet coffee out of Mrs. McCuskey's wedding china. Beautiful she was, on that wooden farm wagon seat, sitting gracefully and lightly in the way I imagine Violet must be sitting today, our mother.

And mother was beautiful—the sum of all she was, was beauty. In her white low-waisted dress with the embroidery down the left side of the skirt. In the dress she wore to powwows, black cotton with red tape trim, cones rolled from snuff can covers sewn on the hem, the pleasant jingle they made as she walked and as she danced next to her dear friend Lisette, off to the side of the powwow circle, the way all the ladies did in those days, swaying ever so slightly, swiveling slowly, nine steps left, nine steps right. Lisette, she was called, and Mother was called Shonnud. Lisette was a maple tree, strong and stately, Shonnud an aspen that trembled to the music that moved the still air.

Like Ojibwe ladies should, Mother and Lisette dressed modestly. All that showed were their faces, hands, arms below the elbow, and their necks, Mother's long and thin, Lisette's rounded and strong. Mother wore a black velvet jacket over her dress, beaded with flowers and vines on the front and back and white scallops on edges of its short sleeves. They both wore lisle stockings and moccasins with flowers beaded on the toes. Their dancing was hard work, controlled, disciplined, and prayerful; their calves were trim and very firm from this dancing, their feet muscular. And I watched them and waited for the day that I would be a young lady in a black dress and beaded jacket, waited and watched them dance as they had since they were young ladies, Shonnud and Lisette dancing side by side, dipping gracefully in a rhythm deeper in the hearts and souls of women than the drumbeat.

It was the following summer that Mother disappeared for good, leaving one day and not coming back the next, or two days later, or a week. Some of the relatives from Mozhay Point came and stayed at the house for a while, and two of her cousins went down to Minneapolis, where somebody said they thought they knew somebody who thought they saw her downtown. But it never came to anything. Dad called the police, but we never heard anything.

We kept her things on the dresser, her hairbrush and comb and the little cardboard soap box with her hairpins. We left her underthings and nightgown in the dresser drawer and her other housedress hanging from the nail in the bedroom with her green-checked apron. We left her good white dress and her powwow dress in the box under the bed, where she had kept them wrapped in an old sheet.

We stayed at the McCuskeys' farm until the year after that, when Daddy died of stomach cancer and the county took me and Sam away for placement. Mrs. McCuskey said she would take Violet, and the last time I saw her was just before Sam and I got into the county worker's car. She was holding Mrs. McCuskey's hand and the two of them were walking away from us and toward the farmhouse, skinny Violet and big-bottomed, kind Mrs. McCuskey, who over coffee and donuts had told Charlotte that she wanted one of her own. Violet's face was turned to the clouds, looking for our mother; she stepped so lightly her feet seemed above the ground, as if she would rise right into those clouds and vanish, perhaps into the invisibility of our mother's arms, except for the anchor of Mrs. McCuskey's hand.

Sometime after that the McCuskeys sold their farm to the county and left the state. I don't know what happened to Mother's things, if Mrs. McCuskey put them away somewhere intending for us to have someday, if she sorted what to keep and what not, gave Mother's housedress and underthings away, or threw them out, or used them for rags. I don't know if she used Mother's comb and brush and hairpins, or gave them to Violet. I don't know what she did with the box under the bed, what she did with Mother's good white dress and powwow dress wrapped in sheets. And I don't know where Violet is.

And I don't think Violet knows where we are, Sam and I. We lived at the county orphanage for a while, but when I turned fourteen I had to leave, because the county said I had to go to work. They found me a job at Our Lady of Mercy, the Catholic diocese's home for unwed mothers, to work in the kitchen for my keep and walking-around money. I finished school right there at the home, with girls my age who were hidden away until they gave birth and gave away their babies for adoption. I shared a bedroom with girls, one at a time, who grew rounder and rosier and shorter of breath, girls who bloomed like hothouse flowers and then vanished. I have seen some of them over the years, on the street, at the grocery store, even sat next to one in the emergency room once, but we never say a word, of course. That time and place is their secret, and mine to keep for them.

I do see Mother everywhere, and Violet, too. Once or twice a month I drive down into Duluth past the work farm and take that road to the horse paradise, which is where Lisette lives now, in this big concrete block nursing home built right in the meadow. Mother and Violet stand by the fence and wave as I pass by before the turn into the parking lot; I spot them right away partly because I recognize Mother's green-checkered apron and the wash dress Violet is wearing, one I have nearly outgrown, but even more recognizable is Mother's stance, that slight turn to her left, her arms wrapped over her middle, and the set of Violet's chin, high on her graceful neck. They wave, and I wave back, and sometimes when I get out of the car I walk over to where the fence was to look for them, though of course they are not really, solidly, there. Vapor they are, the checkered apron and wash dress, just vapor hanging in the air, disappearing as my hands reach to touch. And vapor I become when I go into the home to see Lisette.

She shares a room with a Finnish lady who crochets rag rugs and thinks that Lisette steals her upper plate. Lisette rises above it; that's her way. Last time I was there she had been just minding her own business, propped up in her bed with her hair down, waiting for somebody to come braid it, and Mrs. Kinnunen had looked over at her and said, "You think you're so damn good-looking. Where are my teeth, you whore?" and Lisette had tried to reach over toward the lunch tray to see if the old Finn's teeth were somewhere with the dirty dishes, and Mrs. Kinnunen started to scream. "Leave me alone, don't you raise your hand to me you filthy Indian whore! Help! Help me, somebody help me!" which is when I walked in, right behind the orderly who stepped between them like a firewall that would keep flames off Lisette. He smoothed Mrs. Kinnunen's wild spiky hair, stroked her mean old hand, all shriveled and dried up, that old Finlander skin darker than Lisette's. Mrs. Kinnunen's hand looks like an old peach pit, probably feels like one too. "Moomoo, that is a lovely rug. . . . Here's a nice little bit of sponge cake for you. . . . Is your daughter coming to visit soon?" He waved me past. "She forgets right away," he whispered at me. "She doesn't mean it," he whispered at Lisette. She nodded graciously. "Thank you, young man."

I began to braid one side of Lisette's hair. "You always act like such a lady," I told her.

"That's right. I was raised that way, to be a lady," she answered the air in the room. "When she gets like that I just tell her to kiss my ass." I have to keep my laugh to myself, can't snort out loud. Lisette can't do anything for herself, and how she would even get over to that lady's teeth, wherever she leaves them, is beyond me, but whenever they're lost, Lisette gets blamed, and when they're found, it's because Lisette must have done it, Mrs. Kinnunen insists, hid them on the lunch tray, or on the dresser, or under the bed, and, this one time, in a volunteer's smock pocket.

I braided both sides of her hair and smoothed the braids down past her collarbone, almost to where her breasts might have been if she were younger, wishing that her room was on the other side of the building so that we could both look out the window to see Mother and Violet.

I wish I could reach through the pain that fits tighter than my skin, that I could bring myself to ask her about things. "Tell me about Mother and you," I would say. "Tell me about Shonnud and Lisette." She hears my wish as a ghost voice borne in on the breeze blowing in the open window at the foot of her bed and looks past my shoulder, remembering, telling the story silently to herself, forgetting to tell it to me.

Sometimes I think how it might have been if Violet and I had gone away to the Tomah Indian school, like Ernestine and Cynthia, what our lives might have been like, and what they would be like now. Sometimes I used to think about that even when we lived in Duluth, or at the McCuskeys' farm, used to wonder how it would be to live in a dormitory, have your own bed and a little trunk to keep your letters and things in. To sleep between sheets, to wear clean clothes all washed and ironed, to line up in the lunchroom to get your meals on a tray, at exact times of the day. To know just where to go every minute, and just what to do. I thought of Violet and me in wool Sunday uniform dresses with braid around the collars and chevrons on the sleeves marching with other girls in precisely measured and numbered steps, drilling in formations, marching in time up and down on the Tomah football field while the townspeople watched and applauded. I thought how Mother would just have to take care of herself, and Sam and Daddy, too, all by herself; Violet and I would be busy becoming educated ladies, like Ernestine and Cynthia.

She never came back, Cynthia, never lived with any of us again. She left Tomah with Ernestine, eventually, for Minneapolis, and during the war I went to Minneapolis, too, and lived with them for a while when I worked at the munitions plant. After the war was over I moved back home and up to our reservation, to Mozhay Point. Cynthia and Ernestine never did. But that doesn't mean they're not here with us, along with everybody else, Lisette, Mother, Violet, Daddy, everybody.

See, for me, what I have learned is that we have a place where we belong, no matter where we are, that is as invisible as the air and more real than the ground we walk on. It's where we live, here or aandakii: those of us who returned to the old LaForce land allotment, those of us in Duluth, those of us far away. We were there before we were born and we will be there after we die, all of us, including Cynthia, too. It doesn't matter if we leave, or if we think we will never even come back. It's where our grandparents, and their grandparents, lived and died; it's where we and our grandchildren and their grandchildren will, too.

I learned it in a dream.

Any of us by ourselves, we're just one little piece of the big picture, and that picture is home. We love it, we think we hate it sometimes, but that doesn't change anything. We are part of it; we are in the picture. It's home.

OJIBWE BOYS

Setting pins at the Palace Bowl was repetitious work. To do it took rhythm, but not the kind of rhythm that let you forget about what you were doing and think of other things—that was Punk's advice. A lot of guys had gotten hurt that way, he told us that first night. "It's easy to let your mind wander away, but you gotta be careful. Work with the rhythm but just make sure you pay attention, and you'll be all right." After a while I was able to do that, work with the rhythm but pay attention, yet my mind wandered just the same, and I began to think of other things.

Before I got the rhythm I smashed my fingers and knuckles a few times, and my body ached to where it was just about unbearable, then all of a sudden I felt it, almost heard it, and gave in to the beat. I would be all but dancing to the pattern of the Palace Bowl beat, shuffling, bending, picking up two, three pins at a time in each hand, and over the sound of balls rolling down the lanes right at me and on both sides of my pit and hitting pins and pins hitting each other and the floor as they fell, I could hear that click-click as the pins in my hands touched heads and bodies and feel their smooth cool necks between my fingers. I bent and rose, swinging, using the muscles in my hips, shoulders, stomach, and back for strength, those in my hands and feet for the more detailed work of picking up pins and dancing out of the way of the scramble of rolling wood on the floor of the pit. And once my body began to dance to the rhythm, my mind did, too, and I began to hear it, the melody of past and present, and see the other dancers all round me—Vernon and Punk and Biik in the pits, the bowlers who looked so tiny down at the approach ends of their lanes, Mr. Mountbatten at the bar, Ingrum at the counter, and Miss Winnie smoking at her table, flirtatiously blowing smoke rings—the playing against that the harmony of everything that was happening back home in Duluth and everything that happened before that, too. My mother and dad—he was dead for sure and I suppose she must have been, too—and my sisters, Violet lost and Sis on her own, the federal boarding school at Harrod, and my dreams. My recurring dreams of horses in fields, one brown with white spots, one almost black with a white blaze down his forehead, a round and short-legged pony, an old faded gray blind in one eye, a light brown with eyes as purple and sad as a moose's. My dreams, the same ones I have to this day: Two girls in dresses and boys' high-topped work boots riding bareback in a field bounded by a fence and forests, gripping the manes of their horses. The slender girl sits regally, holding the purple-eyed brown's mane with both hands, her chin high; she half smiles, watching her sister, round faced, with a laughing mouth full of teeth, lift one hand to wave at the sky. In my dreams, the woman in the green-checked apron is holding my hand, her thumb and three fingers circling my wrist in a firm bracelet, her forefinger wrapped around my thumb, so that her dry cool hand is a mitten. "Lookit, Sam. See, there's your sisters. There's Violet, there's Sis. Look, they don't even see us, them girls!" I wave to my sisters, and laugh with them, although they don't know it; the woman bends to stroke my head, which is resting against her green-checked hip, with her bony and tender hand. "Them girls, they don't even know we're lookin' at them, do they, Sam?" My mother, I suppose she must be, before she took off for wherever the hell she went. Next I dream of Harrod. When I run away to Maggie's, I wake up when I get caught by the disciplinarian and brought back to boarding school. Whenever I sleep it starts all over again.

I am an old man now, my dreams the same today as they were when we worked at the Palace, a one-reeler with people, rhythm, and music, sights that play over and over. Girls. Horses. The woman in the green-checked apron holding my hand, bending to stroke my head and my face with her other hand. Her departure. Boarding school. The run to Maggie's. All that was tied up with the rhythm of work, as I danced with their ghosts, living and dead, danced to the silent song of lives led and lives being lived, accompanied by the drop-roll of bowling balls and the clatter and crash of downed pins.

Before we went to Minneapolis to look for work, me and Cousin Vernon lived in Duluth, with Vernon's mother, Maggie, and his little brother, Biik. We'd both quit Harrod school, Vernon when he turned sixteen and me the last time I ran away and those bastards finally got tired of hunting me down. We were ready for the army and ready to get into the war but we were too young, and we were really mad about that. Vernon was going to enlist as soon as he turned seventeen, when Maggie could sign for him to go. His brothers Sonny and George were fighting in Africa and in the Pacific, and his cousins, all of the LaForce boys, were overseas, too. Me and Vernon, we were useless, us, and were waiting until the army would take us, like I said. I was going to have to wait even longer than Vernon because I didn't have a mother to sign for me; meanwhile, we were looking for something to do. Vernon decided that he could stop living off Maggie and we could go down to Minneapolis to look for work.

"I'm gonna get a job, Ma, and then I'm gonna send you some money so you won't have to work all the time," Vernon told her, "and me and Sam are gonna get ourselves a place to stay."

"Mmmm, that's nice," she said.

Maggie, she had us each take a blanket to roll our clothes in, packed us some food, and gave us five bucks, too; that was Maggie. She told us to go find Louis when we got there; he was living at the Holland House Hotel, close to all his friends on Franklin Avenue, the Av, where the Indians in Minneapolis came and went, all the Chippewas and Sioux, Boozhoos and Howkolas we called them sometimes, and Indians from some other places, too. There was all of a sudden a lot of Indians in Minneapolis then, during the Second World War, coming and going from all the reservations, making money working in the munitions plants and factories, living sometimes six people to a room, sharing with people like me and Vernon who came to work, too, and helping out their relatives back home.

We told Biik he had to stay with Maggie and go to school in the fall. He was pretty mad about that, like we were about not getting to go into the army.

It took us two days and four rides to hitch down to Minneapolis. We slept overnight behind a gas station in Cambridge. Early in the morning the owner woke us up and told us to get the hell out of there. We jumped up pretty quick and gathered up our stuff, that guy saying all the while, "I mean it, you bums, get the hell off my property or I'm getting the cops over here," till we were out of his sight. Down the street there was a bakery where we bought a loaf of bread and some doughnuts to eat on the road. We ate the bread while we stood at the side of the road just outside of Cambridge with our thumbs out and shared the doughnuts with the farmer who picked us up.

The farmer took us past Forest Lake, and then a Watkins sales-man in a checkered suit picked us up and took us all the way into the city. By that time it was getting dark but we knew where the Av was, and it wasn't hard to find the Holland House. Louis was back from work, and he was glad to see us, asked us what Maggie was up to and if the LaForces were still up on the reservation or what. He introduced us to a couple of men from up north who worked with him at the grain elevators ('Like you to meet my son, Vernon, and Sam Sweet. Maynard's boy—you remember Maynard") and a couple of Sioux from South Dakota. The Sioux were very polite; they shook our hands and told us they were glad to meet us. Louis and the Sioux said if we wanted to go down to the grain elevators with them in the morning we could probably get a job killing rats. "No rabbits down there; if youse boys get hungry youse are gonna have to settle for rats." The Sioux started laughing hysterically at this good joke on their buddies the Chippewas.

We slept on the floor in Louis's room that night; it was all right, a pretty good time. Louis was a lot of fun, and we sat around talk-ing till pretty late. When we got up early the bathroom was full of men getting ready to work; a couple of the younger men were wet-combing their hair, but most were just washing their faces and coughing into the sinks; their jobs weren't the kind you had to comb your hair for.

We got on at the grain elevators just like that and spent our first day in Minneapolis chasing rats and beating them to death with shovels, work that just wore you out. Our job was to kill the rats that lived in the elevators, some of them growing to the size of dogs because of all that grain they ate. The foreman told us each to pick up a shovel, stay out of the grain shovelers' way, and make sure no rats, dead or alive, got shoveled into the grain that was going to the mill. "We don't want nothing like rats getting ground up into the flour, boys. You make sure that don't happen."

We envied Louis his nice job shoveling grain, where the men inhaled particles of grain dust so fine that it floated like a yellow fog as soon as the shoveling started. Within minutes of starting work the men started to cough. Then they hawked the rest of the day, some of them until they puked, which stopped the cough but not for long. They wore handkerchiefs tied over their faces, like bank robbers. Louis kept his handkerchief tied over his nose and mouth in a square knotted above the backs of his ears and then at the back of the neck. He said it worked for him, and he never puked. He did sweat, though, soaked right through his overalls and shirt, and that fine grain powder stuck to it so that he looked like a big piece of grain himself.

Vernon got the first one, a rat that didn't look like any rat we ever saw before. There we were, standing behind Louis, holding our shovels like baseball bats, and Louis was pumping his arms and moving that grain, shoveling like a madman, like all the shovelers were, and in about a minute this big bushy rat almost the size of a porcupine but fast, man that thing was fast, dodged Louis's shovel and ran right between us. Vernon swung the shovel in this big arc over his right shoulder down toward the floor, skimming right to the rat's path, and pow! That thing was knocked right out; got it right in the face. Vernon raised his eyebrows at me and smiled, then shoveled that thing up off the floor and carried it over to where the foreman said we were supposed to start our rat pile. "Giizis, hey-ey-wah!" Louis called to him. "My son, there. Wait till he gets in the army!" he said to the shoveler next to him, this Grand Portage niijii with arms like Popeye's.

"Shimaaganish, that's him," answered the niijii, and began to sing, "Slap that Jap off the map."

"Wa ha ha, Benito's jaw!" Louis continued for him in a deep voice, to sound funny, and they started to laugh like crazy, working their shovels so fast they glinted and twinkled in the haze of grain dust.

I didn't like killing rats; there was this one that I beaned pretty good but didn't kill it when I hit it, so it lay there twitching and heaving, really suffering, so I had to bash its head in with the shovel. Jeez, that was bad, and there were more like that, too. I had smears of blood on my overalls, especially on the legs; Vernon was splattered all the way up to his face. He really killed a lot of rats, but he ran a lot more than I did and where I got to feeling worn out he got tired to the point he was like crazy drunk. By dinner break he was so wound up from all that running around that his hind end appeared to hover about a half-inch above the wooden bench we sat on to eat the lard sandwiches Louis had packed in the bucket, and his eyes, red-rimmed and teary, blinked excitedly. "You see all them rats? Pow! Ka-pow!" he laughed hoarsely. "P'shoom! Ak-ak-ak-ak-ak!"

"You gonna eat, or what?" Louis asked.

Vernon turned clear around and threw up back of the bench.

After dinner break I looked around at some of the rat killers working with other shovelers, and they didn't look sick, or excited, or even especially tired. They looked like nothing but overall sacks stiff with sweat that dried out and got covered the next day and the day after that with more sweat and blood and grain dust, overall sacks charging and chasing rats, overall sacks holding inside hope that someday they might work their way up to shovelers.

They paid us in cash at the end of the day; we hosed off our clothes the best we could and washed our hands and faces, dunked our heads under the sink faucets to rinse the dust out of our ears and hair, and walked out of there with Louis and his buddies to get something to eat. We had hamburgers and fried potatoes at this bar near the Holland, Eddie's, but Vernon and me were too young for a beer so we left when they started buying rounds. We walked over to the Holland, and when the manager saw us come in the door, he said we couldn't stay there unless we paid for a room, he was sick of that bunch of Indians from Duluth bringing all their relatives in to sleep for free, next one he saw he was calling the cops, and here's your stuff, boys, if you haven't got two bits apiece for your room take it and get out, so we picked up our blanket rolls and left.

We walked a while around toward downtown till we found a place to sleep in a park. All snug rolled up in my blanket between Vernon and a squatty little pine tree I looked up at the stars, same ones as were shining down that very same minute on everybody at home, and started to think how if we wanted to kill rats we could be doing that at the terminals in Duluth. But I wasn't ready to go home yet.

"Hey, Vernon."

"Wegonen, Cousin?"

"Let's not kill rats tomorrow, Cousin; how about it?"

"Okay by me." Vernon was always very easy to get along with.

There was a skinny, worried-looking guy leaning a handwritten cardboard sign next to the doorway to the Palace Bowl. "PINSETTERS WANTED," it said.

"What's that?" I asked him.

"Pin boys, we're looking for pinsetters, somebody to set pins, need them right now. You fellas want a job?" His forehead wrinkles moved up and down, opening and closing like a squeezebox when he talked, his voice high and light. "We had two pin boys just enlisted in the navy, need a couple of pin boys right away. You fellas want a job? It'll be gone tomorrow."

Me and Vernon followed the skinny guy inside. He stood us by the door and told us, "Wait here, stand right here, I'll go get the owner." First, though, he lit a cigarette.

The alley had six lanes and a lunch counter with a bar at one end. It was pretty quiet in there, nobody at the counter eating, just a couple of men at the far lane changing into bowling shoes, and the wood floor creaked as we shifted from foot to foot, waiting. Dark in there. Kind of restful, too, and generally kind of pleasant, was my impression for a second or two. Then I took in my first breath inside the door and my lungs filled with the heaviness of an inhaled large animal, impossible to expel, unthinkable to even cough. The place had a smell that sunk to my chest and stuck in my throat; it felt almost as thick as grain dust but denser, wetter. What was it, anyway? Old wet dog, cigarette butts put out in dirty plates, mothballs, sauerkraut, lye soap, sweat, tired feet. Beer and boiled egg boogit.

But no rat blood. We could get used to that. In the meantime, I just breathed waves of that heavy wetness in and out through my mouth; the taste was bad but not as powerful as the smell.

Vernon was breathing through only his mouth, too. "Dice-lookig blace, eh," he commented. Vernon was always very easy to please.

We could see the back of this big heavy grunting guy bent over behind the lunch counter, replacing an empty beer keg. Skinny walked over and knelt next to him, helping to lift and push the full keg with his long arms, white and dry looking as cigarettes.

"Aaawwrrggghhh," we heard the big guy groan. "Gaaa that son-ovabitch is heavy . . . rrrggghh." Then, "Okay, I got it I got it I got it . . . let go let 'er go let 'er go." They stood up. The big guy had a lit cigarette in his mouth, too. We would find out that everybody at the Palace kept a cigarette going; the cloud of smoke around each person's head really helped with the smell.

Skinny said, "Montie, there's a couple of Indian boys over by the door want to set pins. Fellas, this is Mr. Mountbatten."

The big guy looked us over. "Where you boys from?"

"Duluth," Vernon answered.

"Where else?"

"Mozhay Point, Lost Lake."

"Where else?"

"County boys' home, up by Duluth."

"Harrod School."

"That a reform school?" he asked.

No, a lot worse. "No sir, it's one of them Indian schools."

"You ever been in trouble?"

"No, sir."

"You boys pinsetters? You ever set pins before?"

"No sir, never done it before, but we seen it done."

"You start today, both of youse, right now?"

"Yes sir, we can do that."

"You got yourselves a job. Follow me."

Mr. Mountbatten took us through a doorway at the end of the lanes and pointed at the guy working behind the rows of bowling pins. "Punk. Shake hands with the new boys." And he told us the Palace rules: Punk was the lead; the three of us, me, him, and Vernon, covered for each other; the Palace was open every night; no smoking in the pits; no drinking ever; we had to wear a shirt whenever we left the pits. We could sleep in the storage room with Punk if we wanted to help Ingrum, the skinny guy, with cleaning and anything else he needed done. "Show 'em how it's done, Punk; hurry up before more people come in." He left.

"We got a customer waiting. Watch how I do this. Gotta do this quick. It starts to get busy in here right around now." Punk took off his shirt, rolled up his pants legs to his knees ("gets hot in here"), and hopped over the partition into the next pit to stand crouched, bent forward, to look through the lined-up pins in the window at the man who was beginning his approach. When the man set the bowling ball down and it came rolling toward the pins, Punk grabbed hold of the bar hanging from the low ceiling and half-jumped, half-swung himself up to a bench nailed high into the back wall, lifting his feet and getting out of the way as the ball crashed into the pins, half of them falling right at Punk, back into the pit, where he had been standing. Punk jumped down off the bench and picked up the ball, rolled it through an opening next to the pin window down the ball return back to the man, who picked it up and began his second approach. He crouched, watching the man throw his second ball, jumped out of the way. Nine pins down. Punk jumped down, picked them up, two or three to a hand, and set them back up. He rolled the ball back and stood crouched for the next frame. "Got it? Watch me again, then one of youse try it."

It wasn't too bad once you learned the rhythm, though like Punk said, you had to pay attention to what was going on. It was hard on the shoulders, but harder still on the hands. After a while mine felt like claws, curved to the shape of the pins, and stiff, and they sure hurt, but that kept my mind off my shoulders, which felt like I was carrying boulders on each. Vernon picked it up quick; he always did everything like that, but he was the first one to get hit by a pin when he forgot to get his legs all the way up. Punk saw him sitting on the floor of the pit with his head on his knees, rocking back and forth, and jumped like a pogo stick across three lane pits to pick up the pins. "You gonna make it, Chief?" Vernon's face was all twisted up by the pain and his eyes were half shut with it, too, but he nodded and got up off the floor to crouch for the next frame. Punk shook his shoulder, half embraced him. "You're gonna be all right, Chief; here, keep moving, walk it off."

We each took two lanes, and when they were both full, we didn't stop moving at all; it took everything we had, for hours and hours, even days it seemed; twice the skinny guy showed up with hot dogs, which we ate between games. We drank water from a bucket in the corner, guzzling and slurping from the metal dipper, and kept it up until all of a sudden the place was down to one lane and Punk told Vernon to sit down, he'd take that one and finish up.

The last people bowling were Ingrum and his date, this woman I'd seen through the pin window sitting at the counter smoking and sipping coffee most of the night until the bowlers were gone and the lanes were empty. She peered down the lane into the pit window before she picked up her ball. "Punk! Punk, how are you, honey?" She had a huge smile with a lot of teeth, and an enormous bust, like two bowling balls in her shirt.

"Oh, I'm fine, Miss Winnie. We got two new boys here; like you to meet Sam and Vernon. Friends of mine."

"Pleased to meet you, boys; any friend of Punk's is a friend of mine."

Ingrum told us to come out and sit with him and his friend; the night was over. We felt a little shy so sat at the table back of them and watched them bowl. We could see right away that Ingrum could really bowl; he started out looking kind of funny, sort of running on his tippy-toes, but then on that last step he turned graceful and set the ball down so gently you couldn't hear a sound, his right leg lightly extended and crossed behind his left heel. Miss Winnie wasn't too bad, either, but she was kind of clumsy, not graceful at all like Imgrum, and self-conscious about her dress, which she smoothed and tugged down in front and back every time right after she let go of the ball.

"One ninety-five to one forty-two. Beat the pants off you again, didn't I, Winnie?" Ingrum's eyebrows, forehead wrinkles, and Adam's apple moved up and down suggestively. "Beat the pants right off you! Haw! Haw!"

"Naughty, naughty, Ingrum; and in front of the boys, too." She giggled and shook a finger at him.

She was nice enough to me and Vernon, flirted a little when she asked us where we were from, how we got to the Palace, then started giving us the third degree like she was Grandma LaForce or one of those other old ladies up at the reservation, instead of this white lady big as a man, with shiny red lips and big yellow curls on top of her head and these little drawn-on crescent moon eyebrows.

Where did we live in Duluth, she wanted to know, why didn't we live on a reservation, how did we get to Minneapolis, how did we like Minneapolis, did everybody live in teepees up north. "I heard the Indians up there are wild, just wild. And drink? You boys don't drink like that, do you?" She didn't mean any harm I guess. "Say, did you get supper? Montie, did these boys get to eat? Boys, are you hungry?"

"Well, whatta you think? I'm getting them something right now, Winnie, got some hard boiled eggs left over, and fried potatoes, lot of onions. Here Punk, Chief, Shorty—come and fix yourselves a plate."

"Mr. Mountbatten's all right," whispered Punk, "and Ingrum, too, though he's got some funny friends. You'll see what I mean, but they won't bother you. Miss Winnie either. I say it takes all kinds: everybody's different and everybody minds their own business, know what I mean?"

We nodded; sounded fine to us. What did he mean, anyway?

Miss Winnie stood, smoothed and tugged her dress down over her front and behind again, and waited, giving Ingrum this look, tapping her toe impatiently, until he stood, too, then Punk and me and Vernon did, too. Mr. Mountbatten didn't pay any attention. She said, "Excuse me, fellas, must go powder my nose," and walked over to the can, her backside waggling back and forth, not a bad walker for a woman of her size and shape.

"Wish I had that swing on my back porch!" Ingrum sang it in a thin tenor, a man in love.

She looked back over her shoulder, hands on her hips like Betty Grable. "Oh, you! You are a naughty boy!" she called back with a deep giggle.

Vernon raised his eyebrows at me and pointed with his mouth, so slightly nobody else would notice him noticing, toward Miss Winnie, who was opening the door marked "Gentlemen."

Punk caught it. "He ain't allowed to use the ladies' room," he whispered to explain.

Mr. Mountbatten was all right, like Punk said. He treated us fine: paid us every Saturday night, good as clockwork, right after the Palace closed, fed us a decent meal at the end of each day, didn't mind if we took a little time off on the weekday afternoons, so long as there was one of us there to set up. He kept back a dollar a week out of our pay, which he put in an envelope for each of us in the safe. When we needed money we'd have it, he said; it was a good habit to get into while you're young. By the end of summer we each had a pretty good-sized stack of bills in our envelopes, maybe ten, twelve dollars.

When Buster heard about how we had jobs and a place to stay he thought he wouldn't go back to school in the fall but would hitch down to Minneapolis instead. Maggie didn't want him to go but then Louis went up for a visit and told her that he could bring Buster back with him. She fixed her youngest a bedroll and packed them some food, like she did for everybody who left her house, walked them to the corner, and then went back inside the house to her room, to cry where nobody could see her. To Maggie, Buster was still Biik, her baby boy, her last one to leave and the only one she didn't have to send to boarding school.

Buster was small for his age, too small to set pins, Mr. Mountbatten said, or anyway too small to set pins for pay. He could stay with us if Punk didn't mind, and could help out a little and eat supper every night, but not for pay. Miss Winnie thought a boy that age should really be in school and not hanging out at a bowling alley every night where God knows what kind of people come and go. She offered to take him to her boarding house to live; Biik seemed to bring out her motherly side.

"You can sleep in my room; there's a nice class of people where

I live, and there's plenty of room. I'll put a little cot in there for you right next to me, and you can go to school. A boy like you should be in school, make your mother proud."

Biik was speechless. I could hear what he was thinking, how he wasn't going to sleep on a cot in a rooming house next to some fella named Miss Winnie.

Vernon told her he'd promised Maggie not to let his little brother out of his sight.

Vernon met Dolly one night not long after we started at the Palace. She came in to bowl with her girlfriend and their dates, a couple of guys who looked like they should be in the army. This offended Vernon, who gave his lanes to Buster and put on his shirt to go get a drink of water at the counter, so that he could pass close enough to get a good look at those draft dodgers out with those two good-looking girls.

"Hey, Sitting Bull, can you bring us four beers?" one of the guys asked. Vernon kept walking. "Hey, you! Whoo! Whoo! Whoo!"

"Crazy Horse! What does it take to get some service around here?"

"He ain't a waitress; he's a pin setter." Ingrum had walked over to their lane. "You gotta go up to the counter to get your beers. And we can't serve the young ladies; they don't look twenty-one to me."

The draft dodgers bowled badly—maybe that was what kept them out of the army, Buster said. Vernon didn't say anything, just kept avoiding those balls that the two bums were throwing as hard as they could, trying to knock out the pin boy or break his legs, and lining up the pins that were crashing wildly, erratically, but also sporadically as the draft dodgers drank their beers. He returned the balls as hard as he could to the bums but returned the girls' more gently. The taller one, the one they called Dolly, was better than the guys and had a pretty good approach, Punk thought. We looked out at her through the pin windows and could see he was right. She took her time about it, squinting to line herself and her ball up with the pins, then taking four slow and controlled steps, hefting the ball with her right arm like she didn't use the left at all ('Needs a little more control from that left arm, her release's a little early, but she's got it," Punk said). She looked strong, had muscular-looking arms and legs. On one calf she had a big maroon birthmark. She rolled a fourteen-pound ball with ease. If somebody who knew what he was doing could work with her she could get to be pretty good, better than Miss Winnie, if she kept it up, was Punk's opinion.

On her ninth frame Vernon kept Dolly's ball. He put his shirt back on and carried the ball out of the pit and to her lane himself, showing her a chip that might keep it from going straight, and offered to help her find a better one. It took them a long time; Dolly told her friend and those bums to go ahead and finish without her. She came back to the pits and for the rest of the night stayed off to the side of the last lane, sipping coffee and watching Vernon work without his shirt, stretching her neck like Olive Oyl in order in order to peer through the little window to the pin pit. He walked her home, and she came back the next night, and the night after that, and most nights after that, except for the Monday nights she went to roll bandages at the YWCA and Wednesdays, which were Girls' League night at the Baptist church. Mr. Mountbatten told us we weren't allowed to have girls back in the pits, so Vernon watched her through the pin window. Usually she sat with Miss Winnie at the table next to the bar, where Winnie could keep an eye on Ingrum and all the ladies who she was sure were after him. The two of them smoked a blue fog around their table.

On slow nights Dolly and Vernon bowled, and we watched them through the pin windows. Vernon didn't look much at her when they were talking, or when she looked at him, but when she bowled he stared like he was at the movies. He was fascinated by every single thing about her, that was plain to see: The port wine birthmark shaped like a palm tree, her chain-smoking, how she'd made enough working at a laundry to support her mother before she died. Her arms and shoulders, big and muscular from handling the mangle at the laundry. Her blue sweater that matched her eyes. Dolly looked right at Vernon when he talked to her, those near-sighted, sky-colored eyes seeking and reading in his nearly black ones what he was too bashful to say, squinting a little just like when she was concentrating on the pins. She treated me and Buster like we were her own little brothers, Punk like a friend she and Vernon were always happy to see. She'd never been to Duluth, she said, had always wanted to see Mozhay Point.

Louis bought a car, an Overland Red Bird—remember that car? He got it so he could drive up to Duluth to visit his true love, Maggie. When he got back to Minneapolis, he stopped by the Palace to tell us that a whole bunch of the LaForces were staying with Maggie, but that even with all those people around she was real lonesome for her boys, asked him to tell us we were welcome to come home anytime.

The day Vernon turned seventeen Mr. Mountbatten made a Victory cake in the morning, before the Palace had any business, and boiled up a potato sausage and cabbage for a birthday party lunch. He gave Vernon a present "from the Palace" wrapped in white tissue paper, a wallet with five dollars in it. Ingrum and Winnie gave him box of handkerchiefs. Dolly came over after work and sat with Winnie while she watched Vernon work. It was a quiet night for Dolly. Winnie tried to teach her how to blow smoke rings and French inhale, but Dolly's attention was all on Vernon. She sat with her legs crossed, twirling her right foot round and round while she smoked cigarette after cigarette, holding them right up to her mouth between her first and second fingers, inhaling one right after another, watching Vernon set pins through the little window at the end of the lane. She knew he'd be leaving, going into the army, now that he was seventeen, that Maggie had promised to sign for him.

"Watch me, now, Dolly, and then you try it. You take a puff, then just keep it in your mouth, but don't breathe with your mouth at all. Just stick out your bottom lip a little and breathe in with your nose," Winnie instructed. "Like this."

Dolly roused herself and tried. She was polite, like Vernon, both of them so easy to get along with. They were like two peas in a pod, I thought, just alike. She French-inhaled a few times to oblige Winnie, but anybody could see her heart wasn't in it. Her eyes were watery from smoke and sorrow at Vernon's coming absence. She didn't want to be the only pea left in the pod, a person could sure see that.

So, it was time to get back to Duluth. We gave Mr. Mountbatten a week's notice so he could find some other pin boys. That week Dolly came to the Palace every night except for Red Cross night at the girls' Y; she skipped Girls' League at church. She sat with Miss Winnie French-inhaling and blowing smoke rings while she watched for glimpses of Vernon at the ends of the two lanes he worked. "Pretty soon I'm going to remember seeing these little glimpses of Vernon in back of the pins way at the end of the alley, and I'm gonna wish for that again, wish I could be back here tonight seeing him through the pin window, wish I had that little bit," she thought. "I'm gonna spend my days thinking of him while I'm at work, just like now, but I won't be able to see him at the Palace at the end of the day."

"Hey, Winnie, know what I'm gonna do? When Vernon's gone I'm gonna learn how to knit and make him a pair of socks."

"He'll like that, won't he? Know what, I'm gonna save my sugar rations, and Ingrum can give us his, too, and we'll make some fudge to send to him."

"See this? I bought this bride magazine for when he gets back. It's got all these wedding dresses in it, and things you can do to make your place all dolled up? And ideas for keeping things nice, too."

"Honey, you and Vernon are going to be happy as kings, that's for sure."

"As soon as he gets back."

"That's right, honey. As soon as he gets back."

"And I'm gonna have a baby, too." Dolly's nose began to redden.

Winnie covered Dolly's hand with her own. "You'll have lots of babies, honey. As soon as he gets back."

Louis drove us back up to Duluth, where Maggie signed for Vernon to enlist in the army. He ended up in Italy, somewhere, Dolly thought, from what she could get out of his letters. She wrote to Maggie every couple of weeks whether she'd heard from Vernon or not. After a while Maggie invited her to stay with her in Duluth, and Dolly got on at the Lincoln Laundry DeLuxe, ironing shirts. They moved to a duplex apartment with two bedrooms, right around the corner from Dolly's work. In the evenings Dolly knit socks for Vernon and the LaForce boys, too. When she started to really show and had to quit the DeLuxe she had more time and started some for me and Buster. She read that bride magazine over and over and got the place really dolled up, kept it nice. When we got word that Vernon was missing in action she stayed inside the duplex and didn't go out at all. The baby was born right there in the duplex. Maggie told people that the baby was hers and that Dolly was watching the baby to help her out so she could go back to work at the mattress factory. Nobody believed it but they were too polite to say.

Buster went back to school and got a job at the hospital as a dish washer. The ladies in the kitchen liked him, he said, and made sure he had a big supper before he started work every night. I heard that the shoeshine stand in the White Front bar could use help, and got on as a shine boy. When it was busy, and Emil the main shine boy had to help Whitey at the bar, it was my job to tend the stand by myself. That was easy work: men would climb up the step to the high chair, and I would sit on a little bench cleaning their shoes, rubbing polish in and shining them up. When it wasn't busy at the bar, Emil took over the stand and sent me out to find business on the street, where I would walk around with the shoeshine kit, a wooden box with polish and saddle soap, rags and brushes in it, asking men if they wanted a shine. I'd have to take the stuff out of the box, and they'd put one foot at a time up on the box, and I'd have to kneel. That was harder work, and I had to hustle because I got paid by the shine.

I gave Maggie some money whenever I got paid, and Buster did, too, and you would think with all those people, the LaForces and everybody else, always coming to her house and staying there, they'd all be giving her some money and she'd be doing all right. But that's not the way it was. Some people worked, some didn't. Some gave her money, some didn't. Some shared what they had, and some didn't.

When I turned eighteen I joined the Marines; Buster was so jealous and mad that he frowned and made faces until the kids around the house started making fun of him. One day one of his buddies brought him to a boxing gym to try it out; he took a liking to the sport and showed talent, became a local celebrity. Still, he was impatient. Maggie signed for him to enlist in the army when he turned seventeen. By then Japan had surrendered; he was part of the occupation. We sent Maggie our allotment checks for her, Dolly, and little Robert Vernon. I know she shared what she had with anybody who needed it, including those allotment checks. That's the way it was with Maggie.

I remember a night, one of the times when I ran from Harrod and was at Maggie's, when she lived in that house back of the grain elevators. I remember she had a fire going in the backyard, and us kids were sitting on the back steps watching the sparks fly each time Sonny and Mickey reappeared like ghosts from the dark of the elevator yards with more wood and tossed it on top of the pile. It was late spring and sure cold out; our backs and backsides, too, were freezing, but our faces and hands were hot from facing the fire. Maggie and George were poking into the ashes with sticks, turning charred wood over to find the potatoes that she had set in there to bake. Some of the LaForces were down from the reservation, staying for a while, and they had brought a couple of the Dommage kids, mean little kids we had to watch around Buster because they took his bottle to drink when nobody was looking, and they hadn't brought anything along to eat, as usual. Maggie gave them the first potatoes, took them out of the fire with her bare hands and split them so the white potato inside shone like the moon under the night sky, then handed them to the LaForces and the Dommage kids, too, like they were really important company, like they were doing her a favor eating her food. George bent over real close to his mother like he was helping her dig, and I could hear him whisper, "Why do you keep doing this? They're a bunch of bums. Why should we be feeding them? It's our food, and it's our money. They act like we're rich or something. They're never gonna pay us back."

"Look at us, how lucky we are—we've got enough to share," Maggie answered. "We're rich enough."

The way it was with Maggie is, she always worked; at the mattress factory or cleaning hotel rooms or making baskets or beadwork to sell. She always worked, and so we did, too. That was other people's business, whether they worked or not, she said. Just like it was our business that we worked. When you went to work you could be your own person, didn't have to ask people for things all the time. We could see that. You could do what you wanted with your money. What Maggie wanted to do with her money was to give it away; a person who felt rich enough to do that would never be poor, she said, and a person who thought he didn't have enough to give away would never be rich. "She died poor. Worked hard all her life and never had nothing, but she would give you the shirt off her back," like George said. "She gave it all away."

He was right. In George's eyes, Maggie worked hard and died poor. In her own, she lived and died rich.

She was the richest person I ever knew.

FOUR INDIANS
IN THE MIRROR

Joe Washington watched the three of them in the mirror. Him, Mickey, and Louis. Three Indians sitting at the bar in the Viking, their faces reflected in a blemished mirror through moving clouds of cigarette smoke. "We look like hell," he thought, "especially Mickey. All the smoke in this place can't be good for him."

Mickey's shoulders shuddered and heaved as he repressed a cough. He held a heavy white coffee cup up to the bartender, who filled it again; then he took a sip of coffee, set the cup down on the bar, and pulled a fistful of stained handkerchiefs out of his coat pocket. He retched heavily, wretchedly, into the handkerchiefs, the sound dry, as though he had coughed all of the moisture from his lungs. Joe knew the sound; before she had died his wife had sounded the same way. He put a hand on Mickey's shoulder until it stopped heaving. Mickey took the brown-flecked wad of handkerchiefs off his mouth and stuffed them back into his pocket, smiling apologetically. On the rim of the coffee cup Joe saw a thin spray, a delicate mist of pink. His eyes and Louis's met in the mirror.

"You doing all right, there? Hell of a cough," Louis said.

"Medic!" Mickey tried to get them to laugh. "That's you, Zho! Medic!" His thin, yellowed fingers gripped the sides of the wooden bar stool. Shoulders bowed, he swayed in an attempt to force air into his lungs.

Bracing his bandaged neck against one shoulder, Joe half-lifted Mickey, helping him to straighten up. "Take it slow, pal. Just breathe in slow; you'll be all right."

Mickey leaned against the wounded medic. "Hell of a sight," thought Louis.

"Just got to catch my breath," Mickey gasped, shallowly. "Hey, another beer for Zho."

Louis told the bartender, "Another for our buddy, here. He just got out of the army."

"On me, this one's on me," wheezed Mickey.

"Those black circles around his eyes make him look like an owl," thought Louis. When he was younger, they had called him Waboos, "rabbit." He had been small, quick-moving, somewhat timid. He grew into a tall, skinny kid, long-jawed and cautious, with a rangy loping gait, a loner who loved company. They then had called him Maingen, "wolf," and still did, although as he got sicker he looked like a wolf at the end of a long winter. He was changing again, before Louis's and Joe's eyes, shifting shapes, like Nanaboozhoo, but weak, tired, wearing out. He smiled, and the dying wolf turned into a young rabbit who closed his mouth and became a gray owl.

As if Louis had said the words aloud, Mickey turned his owl head without moving his shoulders, to get a better look at something he saw in the mirror. He blinked, turned back to the bar, then did a double take. He sat still on the barstool, gray owl in a tree, his claws gripping his perch, the wooden seat, his head turned toward the bar, and stared. Louis and Joe turned, too, Joe a little more slowly because the wound on the side of his neck pulled, a cluster of small craters scabbing over, stiffening beneath a heavy bandage.

They saw him coming before they heard his old and familiar step, and although their memories of him were at different ages, they each recognized McGoun, the disciplinarian from the Harrod Indian School. Each recognized in the figure undying scenes from their childhoods at the boarding school.

Louis saw the outline of a shadow, a giant that shrank to become a man lurching toward the bar from a table near the front door, and in the transformation he saw—in days that he had buried but not deep enough—McGoun, the young handyman at the Harrod school, shoving Louis's brother Frank into a pile of manure in the dairy barn, ordering him to get up, kicking him in the side when he tried to raise himself on his hands and knees. McGoun, big and powerful, whose very walk frightened the lonely and vulnerable boys and girls who lived at Harrod. McGoun, the mixed-blood, whose own mother was from north of Miskwaa River, who turned on his own people's children.

Joe recalled McGoun after the tractor accident that crippled his hip, when he was the boys' disciplinarian and walked with a dragging limp, heavy with the left foot, dragging the right, a doubled leather strap hooked over his belt. McGoun, slapping the strap against his hand as he smiled at the boy. "Say 'Joe Washington,' not 'Zho Waash.' Say it. 'Joe Washington.'" Slapping the strap against his hand. Pushing Joe against the wall with his forearm, holding him there, smiling. Spitting the words into his face, "Say 'My name is Joe Washington.' Say it." McGoun leaning, his weight heavy against Joe's chest, the boy finally gasping, "Joe." McGoun, pulling that little Rice Bird girl by the arm to behind the barn, lifting her by the arm so that her feet barely touched the ground, telling her to take down her bloomers, whipping her on the bare rear with that strap till she peed, water running down her legs, darkening the dirt under her feet. That worthless bag of shit, McGoun, who thought he was something because he could do whatever he wanted with other people's children.

Mickey could only see McGoun the prefect, remembered McGoun beating him, young Waboos, in the basement of the laundry building, holding Waboos by the throat against the wall, ramming his fist into the little boy's side. McGoun locked him in the discipline room, where he stayed for days at a time, his eyes getting used to the dark, his stomach to the meals of bread and water, every time McGoun decided that he needed discipline. McGoun played cat-and-mouse games with young Mickey, hurting him physically, torturing his mind, frightening his spirit as it grew from Waboos to Maingen, frightening the entity of the young wolf back into the timid rabbit, Waboos. Waboos turned, kneeling on one knee, to present his back for the strap, at the unspoken signal taught by McGoun. It had become, with practice, a ritual, the prefect looking at Mickey, then from Mickey to the ground in front of him, signaling with a flick of his hand, palm up to palm down. Maingen, the young wolf, fled in defeat and humiliation, leaving Waboos, who was unable to defend Mickey, who knelt.

The shadow step-dragged his way through the Viking and stopped by the three Indians at the bar.

McGoun was older now and smaller than Joe remembered. His gray-brown overcoat was ripped in the front, his face lined; he needed a bath badly. His hands were shaking; he needed a drink even more. The old ghost opened his mouth to speak; rotten breath rolled like snoose between four broken, brown teeth. "Still a sack of shit," Joe thought.

"He's not that much older than me; I never realized that until just now," thought Louis. McGoun stunk, like he had pissed in his pants. He was wearing old moccasins that were damp from rain or piss. The flowers and vine decorations on the vamps were losing beads, like tears falling off the old man's feet. They had been beautiful once. "Where did he get them," Louis wondered. Louis's mother had made moccasins like those for her boys before they left for boarding school, he remembered. McGoun took all their clothes away when they got to school and he lied to his boss, said he burned them, but he sold the Gallette boys' moccasins to the owner of the Harrod General Store. Cheater, traitor. Betrayed his people.

Mickey stared with owl eyes at the apparition. Was he real, he wondered, and he almost raised an arm to touch him, to find out, but found that his hands wouldn't move. He was Waboos, the little boy frozen, mesmerized by the specter. He was Maingen, young wolf hungry for the day McGoun would get his, lowering his head, kneeling at the signal, humiliated and waiting for the chance to avenge his vulnerability.

The ghost spoke to the three. "Can you spare a nickel for a beer?" He passed a hand to Louis, to Joe, to Mickey, where he held it out.

Waboos remembered what to do without being told. He climbed off the bar stool and knelt on one knee, turned to present his back for the strap.

Louis grasped McGoun by the front of his stained overcoat and walked out the back door of the Viking into the parking lot, pulling the ghost who was real behind him. Outside, under the single light above the back door, he pushed the prefect in front of him to the back of the parking lot, then kicked him in the rear, hard enough to knock him to the ground. He rolled the man onto his back and straddled him, his knees on the man's wrists.

"I wish this was a pile of shit you're layin' in here," he said in his soft and distant voice, his mouth inches from the old man's. "I wish Frank was here. You remember Frank Gallette? I wish he was here, I wish he could see you." He hit McGoun across the face with the back of his hand. "I wish they could all see you."

When Joe and Mickey came out the back door, they heard Louis before they saw him, heard his quiet voice talking nonstop, reminding McGoun of things that he had done. Louis's speech was rhythmic; when they got close enough they could see that he was shaking the prefect by the shoulders and that McGoun's head was hitting the ground with the cadence. Under jagged stars reflected in a hangnail moon, McGoun had shifted shapes himself, Joe thought. McGoun had become a rat lying beneath a leafless elm that stood between the three boys and the moon, swaying in the night breeze, moving shadows around the prefect. A shadow cast by his side became a rat's tail switching in the wind; the oily black beads that were his eyes reflected the moon's laughing scorn. From deep in his chest he blew damp, piss-scented breath that steamed in the cool night air. His upper lip lifted, and he half-smiled. He caught Mickey's eye and winked. The hold he had over them would outlast anything tangible.

Mickey was unnerved. "He— he's—" He tried to find words to speak, began to cough, braced his stomach with one hand and stuffed the ball of handkerchiefs against his mouth with the other. With nothing to lean on, he collapsed on the ground next to Louis and McGoun.

Joe crouched, with his arms around Mickey's shoulders. "Louis," he said, "listen, you're going to kill him."

Louis looked at him with calm eyes dark and muddy as the Grand Bois slough at night. "I know," he answered in his soft and even way, and continued to shake McGoun's shoulders and head.

Mickey's cough changed to a whistle, then to a sob, as he tried to force his lungs to inhale. Joe knelt and held him in his arms, arching Mickey's back to help him get some air.

"All right, Waboos? All right, Cousin?"

The intake of air blended with moaning of the leafless elm that swayed in the night wind, weaving shadows around the four.

Louis let go of McGoun. "Let's get him out of here." He put one arm around Mickey's waist and with the other held Mickey's hand across his own shoulders. Joe did the same.

McGoun rolled to his stomach and rose to his hands and knees, then to stand on two feet. He coughed, hawked, spit. "Wha' kinda Indians are youse? Minikwe daa, boys. C'mon . . . let's drink," he muttered. "Get back here . . . snot-nosed coward. . . . Louis, ask your old lady . . . which of those kids were mine." His legs quivered and he abruptly sat. Surprised, he chuckled. "Help me up, boys, will you?"

Louis braced Waboos against Joe and lifted the drunk by the waist of his pants. McGoun pivoted on his heels, waistband held from behind by Louis. "Maybe he's mine, too," he rasped. Louis swung him and he fell, a heap of old clothes and urine. His throat rattled, his eyes glittered and winked, black and shining as jet.

They left the prefect in the parking lot behind the Viking, under the blue-gray light of the moon, under stars that sprinkled broken glass onto the sidewalk, walking slowly away with their love and their grief.

BINGO NIGHT

"Good girl. She's a good old girl, Bineshii. Gets us where we want to go." Earl's car, a green Falcon, was coated with red taconite dust from the road to Mesabi, where he had driven Alice earlier in the day to buy new winter boots, a Harlequin romance, a *Soldier of Fortune* magazine, and a pink toilet seat, like her friend Beryl's, at Pamida. He patted the dash. "Miigwa-yaak, ina? Isn't that so?" Then to Alice, who didn't reply, "Oh, gi-nibaa, little girl. Well, you have a good nap. Bineshii will keep me company; she's good company. Bineshii will just fly us home, won't you, pretty bird?"

He had bought the car used, nearly ten years earlier, from a young guy in Mesabi who had worked on it himself and kept it clean and purring. The shocks were new on that first drive back to the reservation from Mesabi, the engine running so quietly and so smoothly that it felt to Earl as though the car barely skimmed the road, all but flying right over the red dust without hardly touching ground. When he had pressed his foot a little harder on the gas pedal, the sound from the Falcon was that of a rush of wings.

A decade and fifty thousand miles later, after trips every week or so back and forth from Mozhay Point Reservation to Mesabi and back, and through the wilds of reservation back roads to bingo night at the tribal school, age had altered the Falcon's appearance. Red road dust and rust spots had mottled the green paint to army camouflage. The front and rear bumpers had bent and rippled. Because of the vertical crease right below the driver's side rearview mirror (from the time Earl took the door off, backing up with it open because the rear window was covered with ice), the driver's side door closed with a half-inch gap. Yet, Earl thought to himself, Bineshii ran as prettily as she ever had. "You've been a good friend, old aa-da-baan," he mumbled.

As the sun set, the popple leaves along the side of the road let go of their captured yellow-green light, yielding to the uncertainties of twilight, that time of day when seeing became difficult. Earl's face, drawing a gray lavender out of the dusk, peered forward, nose above the wheel, then left, then right.

"Getting harder to see," he thought to himself. "Ye-e-s, sir, she's been a good old car, old Bineshii, the old girl," he said aloud. Maybe Alice would wake up, help him out.

"Hmmmm," she sighed in her sleep.

The road darkened to maroon and curved more than seemed familiar; the popple trees, their leaves darkened to deep green, were taller and denser than he remembered.

Where the heck were they, he wondered. Earl had been certain enough of the direction home when he'd turned out of the parking lot at ChiWaabik Bingo Hall that he hadn't felt the need to look for any landmarks. How many times had he driven that way, how many times had he left Reservation Road for the dirt road cutoff, knowing by feel and habit the direction toward the Mozhay Point Elder Housing at Lost Lake? The blacktop had ended approximately where it felt it should for the cutoff, and the left arm of the Y turn had felt right. How many times had he driven that way, first from going to watch the school building going up, to the day they hauled the pool tab boxes on the back of Buck's truck, over the Res Road? Remember that day, he beat Buck to school, leaving Lost Lake at the same time but gaining three or four minutes by way of the cutoff. He could drive that way from the parking lot of his apartment building to school with his eyes closed, he bet.

Now, though, he couldn't recognize anything they drove past. In the darkening green, damp shapes familiar by daylight began to seem foreign, ominous, vaguely a repetition of something uneasy from the past, or was it of sometime to come? Or was it something from the here and now? Who knew what lived in the woods, that came out after dark? Who would remember what came before, from what memories embedded in not only the stories but the very lives and levels of consciousness, of the generations that heard and cared for the stories, holding them for the next generation of listeners and when the time was right, when it was meant to be? Amanj . . . amanj i dash. He began to remember parts of ghost stories his grandfather and those old friends of his, long dead, no doubt about it, told when Earl was, what, not even ten years old and supposed to be asleep. They were real stories, he could remember that was for sure, each one had happened to a person that somebody knew or to a person long ago, an event so extraordinary that the details were noted and carried by men and women whose job it was to pass the experience and the lesson on at the right time and in the right way. Remember those sisters, with elbows sharper than mookomaanan, who stood as sentries where men younger and faster than Earl bravely tried to pass and were cut to shreds. And what else? Windigog, monsters not alive or dead—half again the size of a man—who craved flesh and blood. Balls of flame spinning across the sky above a person's head. He blinked away a horse galloping toward the car, red eyes, open mouth full of teeth, and ears streaming smoke, and wondered if he should ask Alice if she knew where they were.

"Any gaw-pii left?" Alice, wake up. Wake me up, Alice—was I dreaming? "Alice, gi wi makademashkiki waboo, ina?"

"I'll get you a cup, Earl."

Lordy, her knees hurt, and her middle was too thick to be turning and bending over the seat like that without grunting a little (and her heart ached a little more but only for a second, remembering it felt just that way when she was young and carried the baby, strong and kicking her in the ribs, so she couldn't turn and bend over without grunting a little; how could a person remember how it felt just that way all those years ago?), but she managed to reach down into the cardboard box on the floor behind her to find the canning jar of coffee wrapped in a dish towel and to lift it over the seatback still a little warm and pour some into the tin cup. She pulled a couple of little paper envelopes of sugar from the coffee cart at ChiWaabik out of her dress pocket and sprinkled a little into the coffee, sloshing the cup in little circles to mix some sweetness into Earl's drink, keep him awake and in a nice mood. "Lordy, it's getting dark earlier these days," she thought. "You can hardly see. Almost fall." For years, she had dreaded the long dark nights of winter.

Earl put the car into first and kept it there to free his right hand for his coffee, which spilled over onto his pants when he went over a rut, but those old wool pants he wore were so thick it didn't even soak through to his skin, and the coffee wasn't hot anymore so it wouldn't hurt anyway. When he was done with it she'd remind him to put on the headlamps, since it was getting dark so fast. Lordy, he wasn't paying much attention to the road, more to his coffee and to whatever was going round in his head. Wondering what it could be he was thinking about could just about drive a person crazy, she knew; she'd tried it from time to time over the years. With Earl it could be the color of the night sky that reminded him of that dark blue dress they buried his mother in, then the distraction of the very light scent of skunk in the air that was nice in a way, then the thought of that little rabbit just sitting at the side of the road earlier in the day, like it was in the city waiting to cross the street, lots of rabbits this year, last year it was skunks; hasn't smelled one in a while, just a little in the air was nice in a way. Or he might be remembering how an aspirin bottle looked sitting on the window sill with the light shining through it so blue just the color of the night sky tonight that reminded him of that dark blue dress they buried his mother in, and so his mind walked and wandered. Earl. And him just sipping and swallowing that coffee like he's sitting in a chair in the front room, maybe going to set it down and sleep a little. Instead of driving a car. Lordy, when would that coffee kick in?

"Earl, we keep going west there, we'll hit the Tweeten road, eh?"

He tipped the cup up and his head back to catch the last drop with a little slurp and handed the cup back. "S' good. Mino pugwud." He felt better with Alice awake.

"Earl, we need to go toward west there; we want to hit the Tweeten road."

Earl hummed, hitting about every third note out loud like he always did, so you couldn't know what song he had in mind till he got to a part he liked. "Hm . . . hm, hm, hm . . . hm . . . hm, hm . . . hon-ey, let me be your sal-ty dog."

"Earl!"

"What's that, little girl, Kwesens?" He looked over at her and laughed. Alice, she was always the one watching what was going on and looking out for what might be going to happen, her, so he never really had to; she'd be calling his attention to so many things he didn't even need to know but that was Alice, always looking and pointing things out. Pretty little thing, she was looking some like her mother used to these days, but his eyesight was going a little, both what his eyes saw and what his mind saw, and at times he saw one Alice, or another Alice, and sometimes he wondered whether he was really seeing her, or her mother, or Alice when she was ten, or fifty. Tonight at Early Bird he'd looked around for her, losing track of his two cards when he couldn't see her anywhere. He'd asked Sissy and Beryl, "Where's Alice, where'd she go?" And Beryl said, "She's right there, Uncle, she's sitting right there next to you." And he looked and there was this little old lady with her nose all but stuck to her bingo cards, and he turned back and said to Beryl, "That ain't her." "Sure it is, Uncle Earl, that's Auntie Alice right there," Beryl said, and he said again, "No it ain't," which made her and Sissy laugh a little and he got all embarrassed. When he looked again sure enough it was Alice all busy with her four lucky cards so she didn't notice anything.

"Earl, where's that Tweeten road? Do you know where we are?"

"Little girl, I always know where we are. Don't you worry."

"It's getting dark out. Get your headlamps on so you can see out."

The old couple faced forward, the woman in the blue flowered housedress intent, staring, concentrating on memorizing each big tree and dip, watching for a marked crossroad, the man in the wool hunting pants and plaid flannel shirt mildly watching the scenery, waiting to have his attention called to a road sign or an intersection. He turned to his wife from time to time, taking in her dress as part of the scenery, fading with the day as the lupines did from pastel to silver gray, then to the same dusky color as the upholstery. Her face and her hair, turned to the moon, lightened and whitened, face to silver gray, hair to a brilliant sterling, stray front hairs loosened from the pinned-up braid waving around her face glowing like a row of electric filaments. Pretty little thing, Alice.

Earl always got sleepy when he drove, so she had to force herself to try to stay wide awake, especially when he drove in the dark, and think of things to say. Oh, now wouldn't it be good sometime to be one of those old ladies who slept while her husband drove, she thought. Instead, she had to think of one thing after another that would keep his mind perked up but not so much that he drove right off the road. Let's see, next week was her ladyfriend's birthday and they were going to drive down to the county home at Duluth. What else, oh yes, Earl liked chocolate cake.

"Next week, let's bring a cake for Lisette's birthday. . . . That'll be Tuesday, won't it? . . . You think she could eat a chocolate cake?"

"Sure." Earl peered over the dash, squinting. "You see that old shack there, see that? That look like that old Dommage place to you?"

"Dunno, Earl, amanj. It's all fallen down; don't look like it. We can't be anywhere near there, I don't think."

"Well, if that was the place, I think we're pretty close to the lumber road. . . . Mmmhmm, I think I know it now. . . . Eyaa, we should be there pretty soon." He bent slightly forward from the shoulders and nodded his head up and down a few times to find which he could see better through—the tops of his lenses or the tiny bifocal chips below, small as a child's fingernail—and continued the Falcon's slow and unvarying speed through the darkening dusty road, around curves and over potholes and on the straightaway at twenty miles per hour, leaning the top layer of his consciousness on Alice's voice talking about Lisette's birthday coming up.

"Well, she could eat just a little. I got a lot of eggs, and flour, and that whole tin of cocoa. I could use the Bundt pan, and then I could just put some powdered sugar on top, and she wouldn't have to eat frosting." Lisette. Taking care of everything all the time and everybody letting her do all the work. The matriarch of the family and the whole damn bunch, at Lost Lake and at Duluth, too. Everybody was always counting on Lisette, and now look, spending the end of her life in the nursing home having to let other people cut her toenails and feed her and put in her teeth for company and even tying her up so she could sit for a while in a chair. And with her mind all there, stuck inside that bed . . . that Lisette. She'd outlived a husband and a gentleman friend and most of her children.

Where the hell were they? "I don't think she can eat a lot of chocolate, or a lot of sugar, messes up her insides," Alice said.

"Maybe something else, then," Earl knew to answer, to keep Alice from worrying that he wasn't paying attention to the road. The thing was, he was paying attention; he's always paying attention, and seeing all kinds of things that Alice just plain missed. Like now, for instance, just look over there, just a little to the right, and even though it's dark, a person really paying attention, a person who knew what she was looking for, which Alice wasn't, could see the far end of the Harrod school property, the barbed wire fence that the older boys helped the handyman put up to keep the cows from getting too far away from the dairy barn. And further up the hill from that is the truck farm, and to the right of that is the classroom building, then the boys' dormitory. Or is the dormitory to the left? If he finds where the road forks off to the right, will they pass right in front of the boarding school? he wonders. Or are they already on the road now? It seems to be narrowing. Alice will sure be surprised when they get to the boarding school. She goes to the mission school up north, St. Veronique's, and has never seen Harrod.

"The road is getting narrower, Earl; I don't think we're going to hit the Tweeten."

Just a little farther, just to see if they go past the school. What will the boys think, him driving a car, right up to the front of the school, with a pretty girl. Maybe Louis might want to go with them over to the ChiWaabik, play a couple of bingo games, or buy some pool tabs; they'd get him back in time before the prefect even did bed check. "Ya, just a mile or so, then we'll look for a place to turn around." He slowed, in order to be able to see it if they should go by; be a shame to go right past.

The dark was making her feel a little jumpy. They'd left the bingo hall before the Saturday Night Fever games just so Earl wouldn't have to drive in the dark, and now here they were someplace that didn't look like the cutoff at all, God knew where on this road that was getting skinnier and skinnier so that there was only room for one car, not that they had seen another, and she wished they would. One thing, Earl didn't look like he was going to fall asleep at the wheel; he was, in fact, looking through the windows like he might be recognizing where they were. Lordy, it was getting so dark, and the trees and scrub were so close to the car. She had always craved open space and light; in winter the snow brightened up the roads at night and the trees seemed to recede from the road, but then it was so cold and the nights were so long. And Earl was going slower, but the shadows seemed to be moving as fast as they had been when the car was going faster, in their own shapes and directions, shades of gray indistinct and ominous, brown-gray blending to green-gray blending to black-gray.

And then through the gray she saw color, blue ticking stripes, blinked, and saw it again.

"Earl?"

"Hmmm?"

"Earl, did you see . . . ?" He couldn't have seen it; she couldn't have seen it herself. After all, it had been years. Years and years.

"What did you see, there? Something in the road?"

"Oh, I guess it wasn't anything." It had been a child, a little girl in a blue-striped ticking dress, parting the bushes with her small hands to step through to the road, eyebrows raised and mouth open in her surprise to see Alice, old Alice. The girl's hair, bound at the back of her neck in a long tail, flew in a black arc as she turned to run back into the woods. The little wood spirit's thin back couldn't have been wider than the palm of Alice's hand, but it would have taken two of Alice's small little-girl palms to span it the last time they had met. Alice had not seen the little people, little memegwesiwag, in that many years. She had always thought that they could be seen only by children.

"Earl, I think we oughta turn around, go back the way we came; maybe we went out the wrong end of the parking lot from Chi-Waabik in the first place."

What the heck was he thinking? The boarding school road wasn't anywhere near here. How could it be? It was probably a hundred miles to Harrod from Lost Lake. "Remember," he thought, "you used to have to take the train there. Look, now, Alice looks like she's getting scared, and you're good and lost. She's got the right idea; turn around and go back, start over."

"Ya, let's do that. I'm gonna turn around right here." He slowed Bineshii in her night flight and turned the wheel to the left till he felt the front wheels leave the dirt and sink into grass. He muttered as brambles scratched across the windshield, then put the Falcon in reverse and cut it sharp to the right as he backed up across the dirt, sinking the rear wheels into a soft mud puddle. Shifting into first, he cut sharp to the left and slowly accelerated, stepping a little heavier on the gas as the rear wheels began to spin and whine.

Ai. Stuck.

He rocked the car from first to reverse, first to reverse ("C'mon, girl; come on, old car, you; c'mon"), cutting the steering wheel a little to the left, to the right, each time, as the Falcon's tires spun deeper into the mud on each try. Her wings mud-spattered and dragging, Bineshii bowed her head.

"Jeez, Earl, what are we going to do now?"

On Friday afternoons the Mozhay Point Reservation School let out early in order to give the gaming workers time to turn the gymnasium/lunchroom into the ChiWaabik Bingo Hall. The bingo hall was the school's source of income and a source of employment and pride for the reservation community. Those lucky enough to have been hired for one of the part-time jobs showed up early on Fridays and waited lined up outside the classrooms for the students to get on their buses. Then everybody got busy. Henry and his son Al hooked up the banner grommets to pegs on the wall so that under the painted picture of the school emblem—a soaring eagle with "Mozhay Point Reservation School" above and "Young Eagles—Eagle Pride" below—hung the banner, "ChiWaabik $ $ $ $ Win Big Bucks!" The kitchen ladies started coffee and set doughnuts on plates; the callers set up the table with the cranked cage full of number balls below one of the basketball hoops; the pull tab attendants brought the plastic cubes out of the closet; and the hall attendants lined up the tables and chairs. The janitors shined up the bathrooms and dust-mopped the floors. The teachers made sure that work from every student was taped to the walls outside the classrooms, from elementary classrooms that opened off the lunchroom/gym/bingo hall to the high school classrooms in the basement. Break times at ChiWaabik were important to the entire reservation community, an opportunity for socializing and viewing students' work, for parents and grandmas to walk past fingerpaintings and spelling tests and essays, taking pride in the work produced by the children of their own reservation school run by their own reservation school board.

Beryl was keeping an eye on twenty bingo cards, nine on the table in front of her and eleven in her lap, and with each number called, she passed her left hand quickly across the nine, then quickly, fingers wiggling, flipping each card forward in her lap, right hand flicking the little red plastic windows closed on the numbers that matched the caller's. Her coffee cup was kept filled, complimentary for elders, and between each round she freed her right hand to take a small bite from the doughnut resting on the saucer. She was wearing her bingo outfit, a pair of black stretch pants and a sequined Mickey Mouse sweatshirt she got from her niece for Christmas. Just that afternoon Margie had touched up the roots of Beryl's very black hair, blacker than it had ever been when she was younger, used the curling iron to give it a little body, and teased it up into that French roll that Beryl had worn for the past thirty years, which set off her dangling beaded earrings brick-stitched into monarch butterflies. Her heavy black purse was on the floor in front of her chair, her right foot threaded through the handle and crossed at the ankle over her left. This was turning out to be Beryl's night: Saturday Night Fever Bingo attracted a lot of younger people who spent so much of their time socializing that they must have been missing their bingos; how else could she have won four times so far? Beryl was almost forty bucks ahead, and on the next chair Sis was getting cranky.

It's one thing to be happy for your friend when she wins, but after four times and her acting like she's doing something to deserve it, like she's really good at it, and after all she did really was pick her lucky cards out of the pile, it gets on your nerves, thought Sissy. Sis had had four cups of coffee and finished her (big deal) complimentary elder doughnut, and that young girl with the coffee-doughnut cart acted like she couldn't see Sis eyeing that bowl of doughnuts. There were plenty sitting there but was she going to bring one to Sis? No, she couldn't be bothered, and here Sis always left her a quarter at the end of the night whether she won or not. Well, there the girl was all decked out in her tight blue jeans and fancy cowboy boots with the silver caps on the toes, eyeing Beryl's nephew, Little Bud, like Sis was eyeing those doughnuts, and he was giving her the eye, too, every once in a while, so she wasn't paying any attention to her job, which was to pay attention to people like Beryl and Sissy. Was she one of those Dommages? Lucky to have a job, if she was, and wouldn't have it long, the way she was going. Bunch of bums.

"Pretty girl over there," thought Beryl. "Looks like one of the Dommages, must be one of the granddaughters. She should pay more attention to her job, if she wants to keep it." Beryl knew the girl would never get anywhere with Little Bud, anyway; wherever he went he usually had some white girl following him around, one of those washed-out blondes from Mesabi whose fathers had those good jobs in the mines and who kitty-catted around with the Lost Lake boys, getting pregnant, getting married, having those little mixed-blood kids. Little Bud had two of them, himself, who lived with their mother, that skinny Kimberly with the gold tooth, her still in Lost Lake and still in tribal housing, even after she threw Bud out; you had to hand it to her, she seemed to get along fine with everybody else. And there were plenty of others just like her standing in line, it seemed like, to follow Bud around. Well, that's just as well for that Dommage girl; she was too young for Little Bud and no skinny blonde with a father working in the mines, either, but still she was a pretty thing, and looking like she'd follow him home except for he was staying at Beryl's. She wouldn't keep her job if she couldn't get her attention peeled off him.

"Excuse me, young woman," Beryl spoke in her pleasant and ladylike voice, pitched so quietly that it cut through the smoke and hissed pleas for "B4, c'mon, B4, B4." "Do you think my friend here could have another doughnut?" She daintily pointed her lips toward Sis.

Combined with Beryl's position as the aunt of the irresistible Little Bud, the spell of that silvery voice attracted the Dommage girl like a dog whistle. She listened to the sound, cocked her head, and trotted on her cowboy boots (which caught a little under the back hems of her blue jeans) over to Sissy, her black hair long past her shoulder blades and flashing shiny red highlights, her teeth white as she smiled and said, "You bet," and handed Sis and Beryl each a doughnut. "You want more coffee, want sugar and milk in it, want me to stir it up for you?" She glanced, smiling, over toward Little Bud as she took special care of his aunt and her ladyfriend. See? See how nice I am to these old ladies? See how much your auntie likes me?

"Earl and Alice went home, eh?" asked Sis. "Somebody else could of drove them, so they could of stayed for Saturday Night Fever."

"Uncle Earl likes to get up so early, you know how it is," answered Beryl. "I think he gets more tired out these days; besides, you know how him and Aunt Alice are. They always want to do things for themselves, don't like to ask for anything." Beryl was an expert with her cards, flipping, turning, using that left hand as her guide, never missing a number.

"We should go pick her up one of these days and take her to Mesabi for lunch. Alice hardly ever gets out by herself anymore. He's just got to go everyplace she does; she never gets to go anyplace without him." Sis fumbled, wondering if she missed a G there and, "Let's see now, are we on the picture frame set, or the letter X?"

"Well, you know it's always been like that with the both of them. I guess they just got that close with each other, you know, with not having any children . . . bingo!"

Ai! Five bingos that woman had, and all Sis had was the coffee shakes.

At break time Sis and Beryl walked arm in arm (Sis had a bad knee and needed help moving around till she walked out the kinks) around and past the pull tab counter to look over the display of pictures and papers from the students of the Mozhay Point Reservation School. Sissy didn't say a word, of course; how could she without looking like she was bragging? Her grandchildren's pictures were so much better than the other students' that it was almost an embarrassment. Look at the colors, and look how little

Fawn, just in kindergarten, drew that picture of herself with those four little dogs all on leashes, and those tulips, and the clouds up above, and the sun, too, all with smiling faces. And look how neat she printed her name! Sis maneuvered Beryl over toward the wall by the kindergarten room so that she would be sure to see it. Next to it was a picture with Beryl's grandson Howie's name in the lower corner, scratched so hard that the pencil had made holes in the paper. What crooked letters, and what in the Sam Hill was the picture supposed to be of? A potato? "Here's a nice one," she commented to Beryl. "That little kid sure must have worked hard on it."

"It's Howie Junior's," Beryl cooed. "He is such a sweetheart."

"Oh, my!" Sis started at the beauty of the picture of the four little dogs all on leashes, and the tulips, and the clouds up above, and the sun, too, all with smiling faces. "Will you look at this one!" She peered at the neatly written name. "Why, it's Fawn's!"

"The little sweetie," Beryl cooed in exactly the same voice, "bless her heart."

Little Bud didn't go back to his table after the break, and the Dommage girl was nowhere to be seen after she went outside to empty ashtrays. All the ladies at the table noticed but out of consideration to Beryl nobody said a word. Instead, they so obviously ignored Bud's empty chair that it became the blind spot that the entire table unfocused on. Sis, loyal and feeling generous toward her friend because of the magnificence of her own grandchildren's school papers, turned the attention to a joke on herself.

"I never look for patterns or lucky numbers when I pick out my bingo cards. My system is, I pick the top six cards off the pile, and those are the ones I play."

"Do you change them, then, when they don't pay?"

"Gaawiin, I stick with the ones I pick out when I get here, and those are the ones I play all night; that's my system."

"Oh. So, do you win much?"

"I never win!"

The table laughed.

"Bingo!" called Beryl.

When he tapped twice on the trunk it was the signal for her to step on the gas, step . . . step . . . while Earl, shoulder to the rear fender, pushed to rock the Falcon out of the mud. Alice watched Earl reversed in the driver's side mirror, feeling the terror she imagined a mother must feel for a child in danger. His stocking hat had fallen off and lay in the mud, and in the moonlight the top of his skull shone through his fine hair (remember how soft his hair had always been, like a baby's, silky against her tender fingers when she stroked it), thinned and such a light gray it was almost transparent. His shirt was so caked with mud she couldn't see the plaid; he had torn some of the buttons off when he caught it on the rear fender, so that it hung off his shoulder and swung as he pushed. His mouth hung open as he gasped and gulped in air, and she thought, he can't do this, can't keep on; he looks so old, and so frail.

He tapped once, the signal to stop, and Alice took her foot off the gas pedal. She got out of the car and stepped to the rear of the car, where he leaned against the trunk. "We're gonna try it one more time," he said, then just like that Earl was sitting in the mud, his legs bent in front of him, head hitting the trunk before he lay humiliated in the mud, an old man exhausted and weak and unable to take care of his wife. "Just a minute, just a minute," he said when she took his arm to help him up, "let me get my breath a minute."

He looked so small, and so helpless. Like a baby, she thought, a small and helpless baby. She stroked him as she would to soothe a baby, her special calming way of passing one hand, then another, down from throat to ribs, and felt his heart pound quickly and unevenly, an uneven gallop almost heard. She blinked away a horse galloping toward the car, red eyes, open mouth full of teeth and ears streaming smoke. "Alice," he whispered in near sleep, "do you know where we are?"

Alice knelt in the mud and looked down at her husband, then up at the sky full of open space and stars.

She never saw the baby, never knew if it was a boy or a girl, if it lived or died. She remembered a hand and arm folding her head immobile, a folded white cloth brushing her nose and lips, pressing tightly when she resisted, easing once she stepped willingly into the darkness of that sweet and thick smell. The last thing she heard, those thousands of times she remembered back to what she thought of as her nine months as a mother, "Gaawiin, gego gitaaji ken," came from the boarding school matron, who sat on the side of the infirmary bed, next to where Alice lay, facing the foot of the bed, turned from that ancient young suffering face. The matron had been holding Alice's belly in the circle of her strong arms, pressing her own rib cage down against the top of Alice's belly to help her push that baby out, while her scrubbed hands held Alice's ankles apart and drawn up to her buttocks. "Does she dream?" the matron wondered, and hoped not.

Her baby, born while she lay unmoving and unaware, silent for the birth (how could the doctor and the matron not hear the screaming and weeping inside her soul, the tearing of hair and clutching of robbed belly, the keening that would follow in her wake every day for the rest of her life?), disappeared and was never seen, although she would look for it in the face of every baby, then child, then young person, adult, and finally grandparent, every person she saw from that day who looked to be about sixteen years younger than Alice.

It was at Maggie's house in Duluth where she met Earl, who was down from Mozhay to visit and see how everybody was doing. He walked in the kitchen door without knocking, which was the custom up north, and as little Biik expected at each visit, lifted him to touch the ceiling.

"I'm flying, I'm flying," Biik sang as always.

"N'madabin, nisaye; here, take the rocking chair." Henen rose to rinse and dry a cup, to pour tea. "Alice, this is our brother Earl."

"Pleased to meet you, Earl."

"Mmmhmm, likewise." He was so shy that for the rest of the afternoon he looked in every direction and at everything else in the kitchen except for Alice. He returned every afternoon for a week with gifts for the family: a bag of oranges, a small brown paper sack of white sugar, a pocketful of licorice babies, a half-pound of coffee, a cherry pie from the bakery, and at last a bouquet of chenille violets just for Alice.

They married the following week.

There was no explanation for Earl beyond what she had had to memorize from the catechism at St. Veronique's: God was the Supreme Being who made all things, including the mistake of letting Alice have her beloved Earl. Since the day she married Earl, she had known that one day the Supreme Being would realize this and correct the error.

He spoke softly, as always, in his faraway and wondering voice. "Alice." Earl, looking so small and helpless. "Alice. I think I'm going to die."

Earl, don't leave me. Don't leave me here. "You're getting cold; I'll get you a blanket." She took her coat from the backseat and the blanket off the front seat, tucked the blanket under and around Earl, her coat over his chest and arms. She found his hat, brushed off some of the mud, and pulled it down to cover his ears.

His heart slowed in its gallop, and Earl looked up at his wife. It was Alice all right, though bent over him like that she reminded him of his grandma. What was missing? Oh, yes, her pipe; she kept that little clay pipe between her teeth when it wasn't in that little pocket bag hanging off her waist. Remember how she would smile when she got a smoke, and how she used to suck on it unlit during Mass, when they were supposed to be praying before Communion, bent over with her hands folded together under her nose so the priest wouldn't see her sucking on that unlit pipe. Except for that one thing she raised him the way the priest and the sisters told her to, didn't let him around any of those old devil Indians, sent him to boarding school, made sure he went to Mass every day in the summer and confession on Saturday. And took care of his sinning, too—caught him lying once and yanked him by the arm over to the woodstove, where she held his hand over the burner so he'd get a taste of the hot blue fires of hell and remember for next time so he wouldn't end up burning for eternity.

Because Earl's lips didn't move and no sound came from his throat, Alice couldn't hear him ask, "Who will look for us?" which was probably a good thing, because that would make her think how no matter how much she had wanted babies that hadn't been meant to be. Who would look for them? No children, or grandchildren, or great-grandchildren would be waiting for them at home wondering what was keeping them, why they weren't back from Early Bird yet. Nobody would be saying, "Maybe they're having trouble with the Falcon. Let's drive out to ChiWaabik to see. You take the Res Road and I'll take the cutoff."

His wife looked frightened. "Kwesens," Earl whispered, "Gaawiin, gego gotaaji ken. Don't be scared, now." He tried to smile encouragement.

Behind Alice, the bushes next to the car parted and the little girl memegawens, the one in the blue-striped ticking work dress like the ones Alice had worn at boarding school, slipped through, followed by several other small children, some wearing boarding school uniforms, some in deer hide, one in bib overalls, moccasins, and a man's cast-off hat. They murmured to each other the sound of leaves falling onto the dry grass of an early autumn and hung back, timid of the large and aging Alice kneeling clumsily in the mud and begging the stars.

Her feet above the wet grass, little Alice tiptoed to the kneeling Alice grown old and knelt beside her. "Niijii kwesens, gaawiin, gego gotaaji ken," she began the song, and waved ambe, ambe, to the other children. As the children joined her, they began to dance, their feet above the ground, while from behind the brush more of the little people emerged from the woods. A young man in an army uniform with hair the color of chokecherries parted the brush with his hands and walked softly on beaded moccasins toward the car, his head on a level with the taillights. He was followed by a woman in a long dark skirt with her hair bound in a white turban, who stood behind the children. More memegwesiwag, parents and grandparents, and people much older than that, stood at the side of the road, watching the dance and listening as the children sang to comfort their playmate Alice.

Joining the song in her reedy old woman's voice, old Alice sank to her heels then rolled onto her side to lie with her head on her arm, next to Earl, her other hand on his chest, her eyes slowly closing as her song ended.

Earl lay unmoving, his eyes reflecting the night sky of open spaces and stars.

Down the cutoff road two white lights swayed and danced in unison, growing larger and brighter as Little Bud's truck jumped and bucked toward Earl and Alice and the little people. Angie saw them first.

"Bud, look out! Stop!" Bud hit the brakes and leaned on the horn.

Startled, the small boy memegawens in overalls and moccasins ran into the brush, diving under leaves. The adults took the children by the hands and hurried them back into the woods. The last to disappear, little Alice nodded toward Angie, said, "Giigawaabamin; nagatch," put her finger to her lips, and stepped through a stand of quack grass.

When Bud got out of the truck there were only Earl and Alice lying by the back of their car. The young man and girl knelt, touched them softly. Were they alive? The old man was so cold.

"Aunt Alice," said Angie, her breath warm on the old woman's face.

"Auntie . . . Uncle?" the young man said in his soft and distant voice, irresistible to Angie and now perhaps irresistible to two old spirits about to fly. "It's me, Bud. Come to help. I'm gonna carry you to the truck."

Alice opened her eyes. "Where's your uncle Earl?"

Angie couldn't speak. Bud said gently, "He's right next to you, Auntie."

Alice sat up. "Earl," she said. "Earl, wake up." The old man's eyes stared at the moon, reflecting the possibilities of the starry night sky.

Bud placed a warm hand on her forearm. "Don't frighten her," he thought. "Auntie," he began.

"Earl!" Alice shook her husband's shoulder. "It's time to get up!"

The old man blinked. "Was I snoring?" he asked.

"Earl. Let's get in the truck. Time to go home."

Paul Rawlins, *No Lie Like Love*

Harvey Grossinger, *The Quarry*

Ha Jin, *Under the Red Flag*

Andy Plattner, *Winter Money*

Frank Soos, *Unified Field Theory*

Mary Clyde, *Survival Rates*

Hester Kaplan, *The Edge of Marriage*

Darrell Spencer, *CAUTION Men in Trees*

Robert Anderson, *Ice Age*

Bill Roorbach, *Big Bend*

Dana Johnson, *Break Any Woman Down*

Gina Ochsner, *The Necessary Grace to Fall*

Kellie Wells, *Compression Scars*

Eric Shade, *Eyesores*

Catherine Brady, *Curled in the Bed of Love*

Ed Allen, *Ate It Anyway*

Gary Fincke, *Sorry I Worried You*

Barbara Sutton, *The Send-Away Girl*

David Crouse, *Copy Cats*

Randy F. Nelson, *The Imaginary Lives of Mechanical Men*

Greg Downs, *Spit Baths*

Peter LaSalle, *Tell Borges If You See Him:*
    Tales of Contemporary Somnambulism

Anne Panning, *Super America*

Margot Singer, *The Pale of Settlement*

Andrew Porter, *The Theory of Light and Matter*

Peter Selgin, *Drowning Lessons*

Geoffrey Becker, *Black Elvis*

Lori Ostlund, *The Bigness of the World*

Linda LeGarde Grover, *The Dance Boots*

Jessica Treadway, *Please Come Back to Me*